DEALING

DON LOCKMAN

authorHOUSE®

AuthorHouse™
1663 Liberty Drive
Bloomington, IN 47403
www.authorhouse.com
Phone: 833-262-8899

Published by AuthorHouse 08/22/2022

ISBN: 978-1-6655-6923-1 (sc)
ISBN: 978-1-6655-6924-8 (e)

Library of Congress Control Number: 2022915839

Print information available on the last page.

This book is printed on acid-free paper.

CONTENTS

INTRODUCTION

A long time ago, but not so long ago in another era of car sales, when salesmen wore white shoes, bell bottoms and leisure suits and knew how to dicker. God were they good.

This story is dedicated to the valiant men and women of the automobile business, who will do anything, any way and anyhow, to sell as many cars as possible, with the highest gross profit. We also dedicate this to the consumer, who will do anything, anyway to get the cheapest price possible, and lie through their teeth to get the highest trade in value for their cars. This story is about one average day in the car business.

The time is four AM. A car approaches the field office of Dewey, Cheetum and Howe Construction Company A lone figure emerges from the car, and unlocks the gate to the site. As he's walking toward the door, he pauses and tries to listen to what sounds like the theme song from the Mission Impossible series. I must be going crazy mutters Gooey Dewey, as he shakes his head, trying to get rid of the sound.

Gooey Dewey, AKA Gerald Dewey, anyone who called him Gerald was summarily chastised for not pronouncing it properly. His families pronunciation as they pronounced it, was Garald with a hard G. He got the nickname of gooey because of his love for chocolate covered cherries. He would jamb them into his mouth by the handfuls until they oozed out all over his face, hands and shirt. Originally when they formed the corporation. Howe wanted to be first on the corporation logo, because he had all the contacts for pay offs and good contracts. They were going to call it Howe Dewey Cheetum, but decided it wouldn't really look good.

He slides a key in the lock and slips into the outer office. Moving around the desk he opens the top drawer and the there's a tape, playing the Mission Impossible theme. Oh for shits sake says Gooey this is stupid, as he turns it off. There' an envelope with his name on it and another tape player. He turns it on and pushes the play button. Good morning Mister Dewey, This is Folker Everhart president of Everhard

Popsicle Co. You may have heard our commercials, Everhard popsicles, the sweetest thing to slide between your lips. As you may of heard, I am running for governor of the State of Illinois, and I heard that your company, which is the most crooked of all construction companies. That have taken huge contracts' from the state, for paving county roads, which in fact were politician's driveways. I need your help me get elected governor. I am good friends with the undersecretary of state, and want you to tear up all the north, south streets and highways in and out of Chicago. This will make the currant governor look very bad in the voters' minds, causing countless traffic jams. I know you will make millions of dollars and a lot of money under the table. This tape will self-destruct in several seconds P.S. there is a box of chocolate covered cherries under the picture of the governor and several thousand dollars to help. Gooey grabs the box of chocolates and jambs several into his mouth. As He's chewing them and grinning, the juice is running down his chin onto his shirt. Another voice comes from the tape. I guess it hasn't self-destructed yet, so take a hammer and beat it to death, thank you. Gooey thinks, in this world of mega electronics he should have had an Arab wire it for him. Behind him is the company motto. Welcome to the State of Illinois Where we will reduce all roads down to a single lane or detour it

Charlie Sullivan

The alarm goes off at four thirty A.M. at the residence of Charlie Sullivan. His wife Edna rolls over and shuts it off, as she's shaking Charlie to wake up. Charlie looks at the clock and rolls over, don't wake me up, its four thirty. Edna grabs his arm and shakes him. Dammit Charlie wake up. What the hell you waking me up in the middle of the night for, you crazy women, did someone break in or steal the car. Charlie don't you remember the reason your supposed to get up. Edna your nuts. I don't remember anything after playing cards in the alley, and having a few beers. That's right Charlie, says Edna you had a few beers, yea sure, that's when you bragged about getting cars and selling them cheap. You told big Ed you had a car for his cousin Robert.

Damn, damn your right, I told Robert I would pick him up at five O'clock sharp at seventy ninth and Ashland, I forgot all about it, and the beers had nothing to do with it. Hell I'm getting too old for this shit. Charley was born and raised in Charleston South Carolina. His father Amos had a small repair shop in the poor section of town. It was nestled between two junk yards. The customers would come in and Amos would diagnose the problem. He would send Charley over to the yards and get the parts to repair the cars. Charley found out quickly how to pick the good parts from the bad. Sometimes making several trips to the yards and back for the same part, and getting wacked every time he brought back a bad part. In the late fifties the social climate started to change and there were times that gangs would come into the black neighborhoods and beat up or shoot black people for no reason. Amos took Charley aside one day, listen Charley, things are going to get a lot worse down here, so I want you to go to Chicago and look up my sister Bernice. I have been in contact with her and she would be thrilled to have her nephew come and stay for a while.

After Charlie arrived in Chicago he made the rounds of repair shops and dealerships looking for a job as a mechanic. At that time almost nobody hired black mechanics, because they thought blacks couldn't repair cars as good as white mechanics. He finally applied at Dupree's dealership. He was interviewed by Dominick Dupree, who was impressed by Charlie's knowledge of repairing engines. I really don't need a mechanic at this time Dominick lied, but I could use a good porter and I will make it worth your while to work here. Charlie was hired on the spot and has been there ever since, now known as the head porter. He has the keys to every locked door and is without reproach.

Charlie's driving down Ashland heading to seventy ninth St. to pick up Robert. There's still some guys hanging out drinking their forty ounces. All of a sudden he almost rear ends a state truck putting down Hazard cones, blocking off a lane. What the hell are the state trucks doing in Chicago he thinks. As he approaches seventy ninth St he sees Robert waiting for him. He pulls over to pick him up. Robert slides in the right door and smiles what's up. Charlie punches him in his arm, this is your new car Robert. Robert surveys the interior, shit Charlie this car is filthy, it's got garbage all over the interior. What the hell you expect nigga a brand new car, well you can go out and spend all that money you don't got, and you ain't gonna get shit. Lister Robert this car was well taken care of and it's got no rust. Robert turns on the radio and it's on a black radio station. Hey Charlie this car was owned by a brother, how do I know it was kept up. Robert I told big ED I would get you a good car. I don't care if it was owned by a brother it was well maintained. Robert asks Charlie does the tape player work. Dammed if I know Robert, see if you can find a tape in all of this stuff left in the car. Robert scratches around and comes up with a Junior Wells tape. Oh man Charlie it's got the Hoochie Coochie Man on it. Robert slides it into the radio, and the sweet sounds fill the car. Robert and Charlie ride silently while listening to the tape, finally as they approach the dealership Charlie speaks up and asks Robert for the cash. I know you wanted a thousand for the car, but I could only get three hundred on such short notice, begs Robert. Damn Robert, give me the money, I'm going to hold the title until you come up with the rest of the cash. Robert asks, Charlie how am I supposed to drive the car. I don't want to get thrown in jail for stealing this. Don't worry Robert come back later and I'll get you a temporary sticker. Now get the hell out of here.

2

Dan The Man

Charlie hops out and watches Robert drive away its six o'clock. He opens the main gate, walks to the service door opens it up and turns on the main switch for all the lights. As Charlie is opening up the overhead doors in walks Daniel Maaslov the service manager, a quiet and easy going man perfect for the hectic job of the service dept. Hey Charlie whats up asks Dan I didn't see your car when I came in, I thought you weren't here. Hi Dan listen I'm having car trouble so Edna drove me in lied Charlie. I'll bet she wasn't too happy Dan grinned. Charlie just shakes his head, she was ok with it. Dan walks over to his desk and begins checking over the cars that were held over, for one reason or another. He comes across Mrs. McHenry's name and shakes his head in disbelief. Dan thinks, I'm going to get a phone call from hell. I wonder what's holding up this job. Dan Maaslov or big D' as everyone calls him started out as a service advisor for Dupree Motors in the early fifties. He was hired because of his extensive knowledge of cars. Dan used to build racing machines in his parents garage. He was promoted to manager by Dominick Dupree, the old man, who founded Dupree Motors when old Henry the original manager suddenly died. Dominick liked Dan because Dan could calm down any situation, either with customers or the techs themselves. Dan's still checking on what

4

cars are not done and writing them on to the new log, when Willie comes walking in. Morning Dan moans Willie. Morning Willie, what's the long face for. Shit Dan I still have to finish cleaning up that SUV we traded for yesterday. The dealer we got it from left it filthy, those ass holes never cleaned it up from the factory. Quit bitchen Willie it's not like your working for nothing. I know Dan but I get tired of buffing off the rail dust on those cars. Willie walks away shaking his head, as Wesley Dupree walks past Dan and smiling says Hey big D, Dan just grimaces and thinks some, day I'm going to punch the shit out of that ass hole. Wesley Dupree is the nephew of Dominick and could not hold a job anywhere. Dominick's brother Tony pleaded with Dominick to hire him. Dominick tried to use Wesley in sales, but he would get into arguments with the customers and lose sales. The only thing Wesley had going for him is he possessed an enormous member. Everyone told him he missed his calling and should have been a porn star. The straw that broke the camel's back, was when Dominick walked past Wesley's office and saw Wesley and the customer with their pants unzipped with the customers wife measuring to see who had the longer of the two. Dominick went ballistic and yanked Wesley out of the office while Wesley complained he had the car sold. Wesley wound up in the parts dept. Although Wes has a photographic mind and can find any part without looking in the manual, he just loves to mess with everyone in the service dept. Dan is always frustrated by the wrong parts Wes orders for customers cars, especially if Wes knows their giving Dan a hard time. Wes is opening up the parts department and Dan comes over to ask him about the parts for Mrs. McHenry's car. Wes gives Dan that stare through look, who's car are you talking about? Damn it Wes you know who I'm talking about. Mrs. McHenry's car is that the one asks Wes. You know damn well that's the one says Dan. Listen Dan I think the tech gave me the wrong injector number, and I ordered the wrong seals. Dan just turns around and walks away thinking someday it's going to be sooner than later when I punch the living shit out of that ass hole. Wes calls Dan on his phone at the service desk, and reminds Dan he will probably have to charge back the service department for ordering the wrong seals. Dan is actually shaking with rage as he slams down the phone.

3

Jimmy Dupree

Jimmy Dupree, is the grandson of Dominick Dupree, and it was decided by Dominick and Jimmy's mother that he should get a master's degree in business, and take over as the third generation of the dealership. His father Tacky Dupree disagreed and said he should learn the business from the ground up. But Dominick won out and sent Jimmy to University of Illinois. Jimmy completed six years at Illinois and probably would have needed another six years to get his MBA if not for the palm greasing of his father. Jimmy also tended to wipe out several new cars, because of his partying. Jimmy's at this great graduation party, drinking and smoking some good grass, as he's making out with this stoned girl, she mutters she has to be home by seven O'clock. Suddenly he realizes he has to be at the dealership by seven o'clock. He grabs some grass, bolts out the door, jumps into his new sentinel four fifty five convertible and heads north. Jimmy's mother told him that his father wanted him to run the store after he got his MBA. He's Cruising about seventy five or eighty, got the cruise on, all the windows and top down. He turns on the radio and Genesis comes on. He floors it and thinks he's just like Don Johnson from Miami vice, mainly because he's wearing a sport coat over a dirty t-shirt. As he's approaching Chicago all the traffic is stopped. What in the hell is going on now thinks Jimmy. Well its either an accident or road construction.

He stands up to see over the other cars and he was right its road construction. That's what I hate about Illinois in winter the roads suck, because of all the pot holes and in the summer the roads suck because of all the road construction. Jimmy lights a joint, takes a couple of hits and puts it away. Well if I'm going to sit here I might as well feel good. The station is fading so he tunes to find a strong station and gets an oldies station. The song Pretty Women by Roy Orbison comes on. Instantly his old girlfriend Judy comes to mind, and he remembers listening to this song the last night they were together. They were at Grandpa's cabin making out on the couch in front of a roaring fire just before he went to college. Judy was kissing him passionately telling him how much she was going to miss him. Jimmy slips his hand under her sweater and begins to fondle her breast.

He's confused because her breast is not soft, but hard and hairy. Also the heat from the fire smells like tar. As He's trying to make sense of it all, he hears a voice. Son get your hand off my head, you're in deep shit. Jimmy opens his eyes and looks at a state trooper who took off his hat to reach in and shut off the ignition. His car is nosed up against a road tarring truck and there's tar all over the front end of his car. The driver of the tar truck is laughing and tells jimmy I got something hard you can fondle. The trooper looks at jimmy and asks, son is that a dooby in the ash tray? Dominick gets a call from Sarah, Jimmy's mother explaining how Jimmy got caught with drugs in his car. Dominick calls the dealership and Dan answers the phone. Hey Dan I just got a call from Sarah that Jimmy's in jail, he got caught with drugs in the car. Ok Dom where's he at? Dominick replies he's in the Markham lockup, send someone over to bail him out and find out where the car is so we can get it before it's completely stripped out. Ok Dom I'll get right on it. Hey Charlie you got to go over to the Markham court house and bail out Jimmy. Dan what the hell did he get himself into this time. Shit Charlie he was stopped and he had drugs in the car. I'll get you some cash from Tacky's office to bail him out. While you're there find out which pond the car is in. Dan listen I don't have my car, can I put a plate on a used car to pick him up. No Charlie use my demo and tosses his keys to Charlie. Dan goes to Tacky's office, opens the safe and gives Charlie a grand. Hey Charlie make sure you find out where the car is. Ok Dan I'm on it. As Charlie is getting into Dan's demo Matt Kelly pulls up, hey Charlie where you going? Charlie explains he's going to bail out Jimmy. Matt asks, ok Charlie what did he do now, wipe out another new car. No Matt he got caught with drugs in the car. Matt shakes his head and laughs, when is this ever going to end.

4 CHAPTER

Matt Kelly

Matt was originally hired about six years ago to be a counter man in the parts department. He had a good personality and got along well with the mechanics and customers. Unfortunately he did not get along with Wesley. Sometimes he would order parts for a customer or a car in the shop and if Wesley didn't like the customer he would change the order. Matt would wind up looking like he didn't know what he was doing in the eyes of the customer. Finally one very bad day Matt gave Tacky his two week notice. Tacky starts to holler at Matt, listen you're too good of an employee to just leave. I think I know what's going on between you and that dick head nephew of mine. Hold on Matt and let me talk to Dan. Tacky calls Dan to come to his office for a conference.

Matt asks Tacky if he should leave and wait until he discusses the situation with Dan. Tacky waves him off and says, listen I want you in on the discussion. Dan comes in and right off Tacky tells him that Matt wants to quit. Dan asks Matt if he offered him a position in the service dept., would he consider staying. A big smile spreads across Matts face. Hell I would be grateful for the chance to work with you. Dan looks at Tacky well what do you think. Tacky slaps Matt across the back, I guess you're in service. Now get the hell out of my office. Afterword's Tacky calls in Wesley and tells him that Matt is going to the service dept. He wants Wes to hire someone he can get along with and does he have someone in mind. Wes says he could hire his wife's younger brother Ziggy. Tacky looks at Wes and asks what's a Ziggy. Oh sorry Tacky his real name is Gustofis Zigganopolis. Ok Wes we'll call him Ziggy as he's shaking his head and trying not to laugh.

Melvin Tacky Dupree & Kimmy

Melvin Tacky Dupree, Tacky did not get his nickname because he was tacky he got it when he was eleven years old. He used to hang around the service department and get parts for the mechanics. Occasionally he would help a mechanic and that is one of the reasons he is so much into the service end of the business. One day he was in the body shop and they were painting a complete car. The painter had just finished putting a coat of paint on the car, and asked Melvin to tell him when the paint became tacky enough to put another coat on. Melvin calls the painter several minutes later and says ok the paint is tacky. The painter goes into the spray booth and almost shits his pants.

The entire car is full of finger prints. The painter screams at Melvin, why are there finger prints over the entire car. Melvin gives him a dumb look, how else was I supposed to find out if the paint was tacky, unless I touched it. From then on when he would come to the service dept. the guys would tease him. Hey here comes that tacky kid, and the name just stuck. Its seven thirty and Tacky walks through the service dept. Hey big D what's going on I didn't see your demo and got worried. Sorry Tacky Charlie needed it to bail out Jimmy. Oh ya that kid is going to drive me to the grave. What happened to Charlie's car. I don't know Tacky, he said he has car trouble and Edna had to drive him in. I'll bet she just loved that. Ok Dan and by the way how's business look. Pretty good Tacky were ready to open and I see a nice line of cars outside. Dan and Matt begin writing up customers cars, Charlie and Nick begin spotting cars according to Matt's instructions. Some cars are going straight to a Tech, if the repairs are small like an oil change or maybe replacing a light bulb and things like that. Some cars are moved outside if the customer was just dropping off the car.

About this time Al Foster is bringing in his car for some warranty repairs Al Just had an operation on his eyes and his niece Kimmy is driving the car. As soon as they get into the service dept, Kimmy tells Al she is in serious distress because she was at a party last night and all the beer she drank is now coming out of the wrong place, along with the hard boiled eggs she ate. Kimmy needs the bathroom desperately. She jumps out immediately and heads for the bathroom. Al gets out and Matt comes over to help him to the service counter. Dan asks hey Al when do you think the bandages will be coming off? Al says I think they will be coming off in about a week, and Dan thank god they gave me the seeing eye dog. Meanwhile Al's seeing eye dog jumps over to the front seat and puts his paws on the steering wheel. Dan looks at the car, it needs to be moved up so other cars can get into the service dept. Dan hollers to Nick, Hey move that car up. Nick goes over to the car and seeing the dog behind the steering wheel thinks wow they can really teach those German Sheppard's all kind of things, so he gets in the passenger seat and tells the dog ok you drove it in so drive it out. Dan can't believe what he seeing and walks over to the drivers door and removes the Sheppard. Now dammit Nick move the car. As he's walking back to give the dog to Al, he thinks that kid is about as smart as a box of rocks.

Kimmy hits the showroom as fast as she can while trying to keep her butt as tight as possible. She runs right into Elk the sales person and almost knocks him over. Could you show me where the bathroom is while kind of hopping around. No problem young lady it's right over there. Kimmy bolts to the door, but it's locked. Elk says someone must be in there. Kimmy begs is there another bathroom in the showroom. Come on I think you could use the bosses personal bathroom and leads her to Tacky's office. Hey boss this young lady is in need of a bathroom. Tacky looks up from his desk, and says what about the one in the showroom. Kimmy answers sir someone is using it and I really need to go. Tacky smiles and says go ahead use my bathroom, in reality it's because she is so cute and definitely in need of a toilet. Kimmy hits the bathroom and it sounds like a bomb just went off. Tacky and Elk both are startled and they start laughing, Elk that much gas could kill a crowd of people. After several minutes Kimmy comes out blushing beet red. She says thank you sir, I really appreciated your help. Tacky says oh don't worry about it, we all have had our moments, with a big grin on his face. After Kimmy leaves Tacky tells Elk you better get the deodorizing spray, it has to smell like hell in there. Elk sticks his head into the washroom and exclaims, Tacky I don't believe it, this smells like roses in here. I'll bet she lives in Oak Brook. Tacky comes over and gives it a whiff. No Elk definitely north shore. They both give it another whiff, you know there's a certain piquant about it I'll bet its Oak Park. Tacky inhales deeply, your right it is Oak Park.

6 CHAPTER

Eldon Elk Kendale

Eldon Elk Kendale didn't get his nick name because of his initials Elk is about four hundred pounds. He's as wide as he is tall, sports a good head of shaggy hair and a full beard. When he's in his office he looks like a Hugh St Bernard He has a very mellow disposition. Women like him because he doesn't hit on them, and husbands like him because he's no threat to their masculinity. Elk sells a lot of cars because he's so smooth, but that doesn't mean he's isn't kinky. Several years ago they hired a girl for the office, her name was Penny. One morning she was handing out the commission sheets. As she entered Elks office he inquired did she save enough money to get her boyfriend a nice present for his birthday. Penny just shakes her head, Elk I want to get him something really nice, because he treats me the best all the time. Elk smiles and looks her up and down. Penny how would you like to make a thousand dollars. She responds Elk you big fat pig, do you think I would have sex with you. I wouldn't do that for a million dollars. Penny I don't want to have sex with you. Oh Elk I'm sorry I said that, Please don't be mad at me. Not to worry Penny I wouldn't have sex with you. I want you to have sex with Wesley I just want to watch. Penny throws his commission sheet at him and storms out of his office. Penny almost runs into Mike as she's leaving Elk's office. Mike smiles I heard that, Elk you are one kinky SOB. Both of them start laughing.

Jimmy Gets Ripped

Finally around ten o'clock Charlie comes in with Jimmy in tow, and drags him to Tacky's office. Tacky just looks down with a bad frown on his face. Finally after several minutes Jimmy starts to say something, Tacky lifts his arm up to shut up Jimmy, and finally looks up. You ass hole you have to take after your mother's side of the family. You have cost me almost one hundred grand, not counting today. Charlie how much did it cost me today to get this dick head out of jail. Well Mr. Tacky the judge set bail at twenty thousand, but I told him I only had one thousand.

The judge asked me if I worked for Dupree motors, and I told him I did. He said he thought that Jimmy's name sounded familiar. He looked at Jimmy, listen kid I've bought many a new car from your father and grandfather. They always treated me right. I'm going to lower the bond to ten thousand, and you better stay out of trouble. Tacky slowly smiles ok screw it lets get to work. Jimmy smiles hey old man when am I going to start running things around here. Tacky jumps up grabs an ash tray and almost throws it at Jimmy. You little shit you're going to start just like everyone else, get out there and sell cars. Hey pops I got an MBA in business administration, and I know how to run businesses. Tacky laughs ok you got an MBA I don't give a shit, if you got an MBA or an

MBB all you know is how to party. Now get your ass out there and sell cars, because you don't get another dime from me unless you produce. Thank god I didn't have more kids. After Jimmy leaves Tacky's office Charlie hangs around. Something I can do for you asks Tacky. Yes Sir Mr. Tacky you see the car I bought from you last month, well the tranny went out. I talked to Dan and he told me to bring it in to see what they can do. Last night we took in this old Chevy on trade for three hundred. I figured it would be cheaper to buy that than fix the trans. I took the liberty to take it home and show the wife. She liked it right off so I was wondering how much I could buy it from you.

Oh Hell Charlie I'm sorry about the trans going out on that car you just bought from me last month. I wouldn't want to screw anybody that works for me. You can buy it for a hundred, I would rather lose a couple of hundred than have you dissatisfied with the place you work at. Have Tricky bill it out, and thank you for getting Jimmy plus you saved me a thousand bucks. I really appreciate that Mr. Tacky, you're a super boss. Hey Charlie if Nick and Jose are finished spotting cars in service. Have them come up here and dust off the showroom cars.

8 CHAPTER

The Salesmen

Besides Elk in sales there's also Tony Farina the sales manager his brother Alfonso, Mike Stevens. Faruk Maroqus, Tim Polsivolka and Felix Washington. This comprised the complete new car sales force. They also sold the used cars, because the used car volume was not high enough to have a separate department. Tony Farina appraised all trade in's and separated the cars that would checked by Louey, the used car mechanic, or wholesaled. Al and Tony were like a tag team. When Al got someone in his office and they were negotiating the price Tony would stand in the doorway and not let the customer out until they had a deal.

Today Mike is also having a bad day, that's why Kimmy couldn't get into the washroom. It seems his wife made some killer chili for dinner last night and his stomach is paying the price. Mike gets the urge again and heads for the bathroom, which is by the customer waiting room. The door is locked and he is squirming to hold it in. The TV is on and there's a commercial about diarrhea. The announcer is talking how the product will prevent loose stool. The bathroom opens and Mike heads in there to relieve himself. In the meanwhile a customer changes channels to a home repair channel. As Mike exits the bathroom he hears the announcer state If you want to fix that loose stool you need Stan's heavy duty fixit available in the hardware section of your local supermarket. Mike thinks that's got to be some good shit if their selling it in the hardware section.

Jimmy's Score

Jimmy's standing in the middle of the showroom looking around. The sales force are either talking or on the phone and drinking coffee. As he turns around a custom van pulls up, the doors open and an Indian family gets out. Jimmy wonders which sales person should be greeting these people. As he looks back in the showroom there are no sales people it's completely vacant. Jimmy thinks that's strange, why would they leave. The older man walks up to Jimmy and announces himself as Dr. Patal and he is purchasing a car for his sister. The doctor tours the showroom and stops at the top of the line sedan, the Sentinel 455. Jimmy tells the doctor that he is a Dupree and can give him a really good deal. The list price is forty six thousand, how will, the good doctor be paying for the car.

Doctor Patal smiles, I am not purchasing this car for myself. My sister is buying the car and I will give you fifteen thousand cash. I am a serious buyer and I will take this car home today. Jimmy is perplexed if the car is for your sister why doesn't she come in and purchase it herself. Dr. Patal frowns, you don't understand my sister is a stupid women. She might pay the full list price. Jimmy can't believe what he's hearing and asks, your sister is stupid, how terrible to call your sister a name like that. Dr. Patal holds his hands up, no, no my sister is an anesthesiologist, she just doesn't know how to buy a car. Jimmy tells the doctor that he has to find out how much he can sell the car for. The doctor tells Jimmy you told me you owned this dealership. Jimmy shakes his head no my dad owns it, I'm sorry I gave you the wrong impression, as he slowly backs away from the doctor. Tacky is standing in the doorway of his office and was watching Jimmy flopping around like a beached whale. Jimmy pleads, dad I need your help.

Mike's Ride

Meanwhile Mike is leaning over a convertible in the showroom, thinking about his rear end problems. Two very young girls approach the convertible and ask Mike if they could take it for a ride. Mike's hesitant, but when they sit in the car their short skirts slide up to reveal transparent underwear. I'm sorry girls but I have to get authorization from the sales manager. Mike goes to Tony and tells him he doesn't want to tell the girls no to their request because of they are so cute. Tony says oh go ahead and give them a ride in a convertible from the lot. The girls have been wiggling around in the front seats pretending they were driving the car. Mike pulls up a new convertible from the lot and comes in to the showroom, where he gathers the girls up and leads them to the car outside. Tacky is trying to help Jimmy with his first customer. Jimmy listen you have probably the world's best negotiators I want you to start at list price and as the customer gives you a price he wants to pay, you counter by slightly lowering the price of the car.

While he's instructing Jimmy, the porters have been wiping down the cars in the showroom and as soon as the girls leave to drive the convertible, both Nick and Jose open the doors to the convert and begin sniffing the front seats. The sniffing gets so loud that both Tacky and Jimmy are distracted. Finally Tacky walks over to the porters and grabs Nick while hollering for both to get the hell out of there and do something constructive. Jimmy goes back to the doctor and tells him that it would be a good idea to have his sister come in and at least look at the car he is proposing for her. The one in the showroom is fire engine red and the doctor's sister would most likely want something more conservative. Dr. Patal agrees with Jimmy and tells him his sister is waiting in the van for him to seal the deal. Jimmy from right out of nowhere tells the doctor I think you should bring in your sister so she can pick out the car she wants, and you and I can negotiate the price. The doctor pauses for several moments, then complements Jimmy.

You are right, my sister should be able to pick the car she wants, and after all it's not like picking a husband. The doctor brings in his sister and introduces her to Jimmy. Young sir Jimmy this is my sister Enieda, you can refer to her as Dr. Enieda. Jimmy smirks, are you in need of a car. Enieda looks up and frowns, many people have used my name in fun. Jimmy realizes he really screwed up. I hope you don't take this in a bad way, I was just messing around. I'm sorry if I offended you. The doctor starts laughing, that's not the worst things men have said regarding her name.

Mike is taking the girls for a demonstration drive in the new convertible. He positions himself in the middle of the back seat, so he can point out all the options of the new car. They drive down to the next light and are going to make a left turn. They pull up to the red light, in the other lane is a landscaping truck. The truck is what is called a stake bodied truck because it has wooden sides in back of the cab. There are several Hispanics sitting in the rear part of the truck. When the convert pulls up next to them, they all get up and start hollering, hey puta, hey puta and begin sticking out their tongues and wiggling them. Mike looks up, and because he's so kinky, says oh look girls those guys are waving at you with their tongues, what does that mean.

Both girls look back and at each other with a disgusted look on their face, and then start to laugh, but things are not going smoothly for Mike, he ripped a real wet one on this ride and needs to get back to the bathroom ASAP.

11

What No Blond

Things are going smoothly in the service department when an exotic dancer pulls her car into service. Dan walks over to the car and asks, young lady what can I do for you. She says I'm bringing in my car to trade it in. My boyfriend gave me this car, it used to belong to another dancer and I don't want it. Well you will have to take it to the sales department, this is the service department. She looks up at Dan I don't have time to discuss this. You will have to deal with it. She opens the door pushing Dan backwards, and as she is getting out her skirt slides up. Dan glances down with a look of bewilderment on his face. I didn't know they made black wool underwear.

She frowns, don't be silly I'm an exotic dancer, I don't wear underwear. Well young lady aren't you a-a blond. She shakes her head, how do I get to the showroom. Dan shows her the door to the showroom. As Dan gets back to his desk, he tells Matt I can't believe how these young girls walk around. Matt Laughs Dan you are so old fashioned. Mike left the girls sitting in the convert and is heading for the bathroom through the service department. Dan hollers Mike can you pull up that car. Mike gets in the car and rips off another one, so he jumps out without pulling it up. So Dan tells Nick pull up that car. Nick heard the remark about the exotic dancer, so he opens the door

23

and plants his nose on the front seat, inhaling deeply. The smell is like a lightning bolt through his senses. Nick reals around and throws up into the service drain.

Tony sees that Mike left the convertible leaving the girls sitting there. He walks over to the car and asks the girls how they liked the ride. Both girls pipe up and say how much they like the car but they don't have a lot of credit to buy the car. Well girls are you both over the age of eighteen. They both nod yes. O.K. girls if you really want to drive the car I might be able to work something out where you could drive it for free. The girls ask how is that possible. Tony takes out his business card, writes his address on it and tells them to come over to his house later tonight, when they get there he will fill in the details, and maybe some other things.

12 CHAPTER

What A Deal

Maury Silverstone comes to Tackys' office. Tacky you know that my bank has been trying forever to get your business. Tacky frowns listen Maury your rates are too high, in this part of town we have regular working people. Not like on the north side where all you bankers live. Listen Tacky I agree our south side branch is losing money because we don't have any income from the south side residents. I would like to get your business and I would lower our rate to you if you agreed to send me some business. Ok a rate reduction would be great, but how do I know if you're for real. Listen Tacky the first five deals you send me I will approve. I don't care if they have any credit, or if they even have a driver's license. Tacky smirks ok you got a deal. Send over the agreement, signed and I will sign and send back.

Tim Polsivolka is walking the used car lot because sometimes the neighborhood kids break into the cars and party or steal the radios. He bumps into Jose who came out to wash the used cars. Hey Joe what's up you look kind of down? Oh Mister Tim I don't know what to do, my girlfriend and the mother of my daughter wants to go back to Mexico and visit her mother. I don't have a car that could make the trip. The gang bangers have been talking to her and saying that they would be happy to take her to Mexico. I'm worried that they would sell her into prostitution, and I would never see her again. Oh god Jose that's terrible maybe I could talk to tricky Dick he might be able to help you. Mister Tim I would be forever your friend if you could help me. You know Jose the factory has a promotion of a new cell phone on every SUV. Oh Mister Tim if you could help me I would send my girls sister over to really take care of you. Tim thinks for a minute I have seen Jose's sister in law she weighs over four hundred pounds. She saw you a while back and really likes you. You and she could have a wild time together. Tim only weighs one hundred and sixty five pounds. Shit I don't want to die from suffocation Thanks Jose just making you happy would be enough.

Jack Moran is going over his finances, I can't believe this, and my credit is going down the toilet. Jack's been laid off over a year and a half. His unemployment ran out several months ago. What's really bad is his wife spends money like there's no tomorrow, and to make matters worse he promised his son Brian that when he reached his eighteenth birthday he would cosign for a car. Jack's not really worried because even if he could cosign Brian doesn't make enough money to afford a new car. Brian works at the local SUDS & DUDS He only makes about eight bucks an hour.

Today is Brian's birthday and Jacks waiting for the big question? Brian is on top of the world. Today is his birthday and daddy promised to cosign for a new car oh yaa. Hey dad you know what day this is. Happy birthday Brian, Jack comes over and shakes Brian's hand. Dad were going to go and get me that car you promised you would get me when I turned eighteen. I'm sorry Brian I can't cosign for a car for you because I don't have a job. Besides how much money have you put away for a down payment on any car? Come on dad you know I don't have a down payment, but Dupree's has a no down payment sale going on right now. Listen Brian you don't make enough money working at the DUDS & SUDS to be able to make payments on a car. Dad screw you and go to hell you don't know how much I was looking forward to having a car of my own, instead of driving that shit box of yours. I'm going down to Dupree's and buy my own car. Ok kid knock yourself out.

The finance manager is Richard Dixon but everyone calls him Tricky Dick. He handles all the sales closing and paperwork from all sales. He also does all the financing. The banks that he finances through have what they call a buy rate. If the rate that the bank charges is seven percent and Tricky Dick charges the customer nine percent then the difference is profit for the company. After he has billed out a customer and made a substantial profit he would stand up put up his arms with his fingers in a victory salute, and says I am not a crook while laughing. The Indian family that Jimmy has been working with are in the far corner. Tacky just stands there and grins, this kid is going no where. He can see Dr Patal waving his arms and his sister is leaning over and whispering to Jimmy. Several minutes later Jimmy comes up to Tacky and shows him what they agreed on. I'm sorry dad this is only what they would pay for the car. Tacky looks at the order, hell Jimmy this is almost full price, did you get a deposit. No dad I didn't get a deposit. Tacky goes oh shit then we really don't have a real sale. Dad you mean we don't sell cars for the full price. That's ok Jimmy can you get a down payment or maybe a credit card. No dad I got a check for that price and I talked them into an extended warranty. Tacky is light headed, quick Jimmy send them over to Tricky Dick before they come out of the either. Tacky's ecstatic this kid is phenomenal.

After Mike left the girls he has this squishy feeling in his shorts and heads back for the washroom. He drops his pants and his shorts as he's sitting on the commode. What he sees is a large wet pile of poop in his shorts, worse than that some has bleed through to his pants. Mike slides off his shoes and carefully removes his pants and shorts. He takes a moment to take care of his butt, than gets off the commode, kneels down in front of the commode and begins to wash out his shorts. He hangs his shorts over the back of the toilet and begins to clean his pants. About that time Faruk enters the washroom because he has to wiz. He's at the urinal when he hears a squishy noise coming from the toilet area. From under the door he sees a person with no pants or shoes on kneeling down. Besides that there are 2 shoes with pant legs draped over them facing the kneeling person. Faruk can't believe his eyes. To think I left my country to come over to a place like this. Faruk makes a bee line for the bathroom door.

13

Mrs McHenery

Dan calls Wayne the tech that's been working on Mrs. McHenery's car over to his desk. Wayne what the hell is going on with Mrs. McHenery's car. Wes told me you gave him the wrong information and he ordered the wrong parts. Dan that ass hole is full of shit I gave him the correct engine size for the injector seals. All right Wayne I'll see what I can do to get the correct parts. Just as Dan is turning around he almost falls over Mrs. McHenery who is about four and a half feet tall and almost as wide. I'm sorry Mrs. McHenery I didn't see you. Mrs. McHenery gives Dan a cold hard stare, what the hells going on with my car. It's been here for four days and you promised it would only take a couple of days. I'm really getting pissed off. The only way I can get around is to ask my neighbor to drive me. He's a sick old man who keeps trying to cop a feel every time I get in his car. Now you listen Mr. big Dan if I don't get my car back by tomorrow I'm going to call the better business bureau. Do you understand dick head. With that she turns around and storms out of the service dept. Dan walks over to the parts counter, and Wes is snickering.

Hey Mr. big Dan dick head what can I do for you, Dan has this sudden urge to jump over the counter and beat the shit out of Wes. Ok Wes cut the crap I need those injector seals as soon as possible. Wes says ok Dan I will call around and see if I can get them locally. Dan turns around to go back to the service counter and hears Wes say to Ziggy, order a set of intake manifold seals for a nineteen fifty three Hudson. Dan reals around and starts back toward Wes. Wes starts laughing Dan I'm only kidding. I'll have the seals here today But I might have charge service a fee to go get them. Dan shakes his head and thinks someday I am going over that counter.

Jose Scores with His Girl

Jose comes into the showroom with Tim, and walks right over to the land cruiser five thousand. Mr. Tim this is what I want to buy. Tim starts to laugh, Jose you can't afford this land cruiser. How about the economy fifty it's a good car for a first time buyer. Jose says Mr. Tim if I come home with that little piece of sheet my girl will run to the gang bangers laughing all the way. Now listen Jose the econo fifty has fifteen hundred cash back and a new smart phone. Mr. Tim I don't need the phone I just want the land cruiser. Ok Jose I'll go talk to Tricky and see if they have one hundred month financing. Tim goes into Tricky's office, and tells him what Jose wants to buy.

Hey Tim send him in I just found out we can finance anyone with no money down. All right Tricky, your calling the shots. Tim sends in Jose and tells him He's been approved. Mr. Tricky I want the land cruiser that's on the showroom floor. I also want the smart Phone and the fifteen hundred cash back. Tricky smiles hey no problamo Jose I will throw in an extended warranty in the package. Mr. Tricky I don't know if I can afford an extended warranty. Oh Hell Jose you probably won't be able to make the payments anyway so take the warranty. Cool Mr. Tricky where do I sign. Tim is on the showroom floor and gets the keys for the land cruiser. Hey Jose do you want to take it off the showroom floor. No problem Tim, don't you fill the up cars with gas when someone buys a new car. Your right Jose just take it down to the station on the corner and give them the stock number they will fill it up. Jose calls his girlfriend and the mother of his daughter.

Hey my little Chiquita are you and my little girl ready for a trip to Mexico. Jose how are going to get there, maybe on one of those stinky metra buses that you drive to work every day. Oh no my little Chiquita I have a new land cruiser five thousand and we are going to see your family. Jose did you steal it. I want to know I don't want to go to jail for some dumb shit wet back. Where did you get the phone that you called me on. I bought this new SUV legit. Those gang bangers couldn't get you a great ride like I just got, along with the phone and a pocket full of cash. Oh Jose I will be waiting for you. I feel so warm I want to be next to you. As Jose is pulling out the land cruiser Tim tells him Jose after you fill it up I want you to get another land cruiser ready for the show room. Mr. Tim, piss off, I'm going to Mexico.

15 CHAPTER

Jenna's New Car

Jenna LeMont is finally getting to the showroom and she naturally attracts the attention of Tony Farina Hi I'm Tony Farina the sales manager how can I help you. Oh thank you my name is Jenna LeMont and I want to trade in my convertible for a new one that hasn't been sat on by a low life. Tony feigns ignorance, I don't understand. I'm sorry Tony I am a dancer at the Kitty Litter Lounge, and my boyfriend gave me this convertible that his old girlfriend used to drive. I don't want it. I can't believe that he would give me a car that was driven by some skanky tramp. She probably drove it with no underwear on and stained the seat. Tony rolls his eyes and thinks look who's calling the kettle black. But he says I can't believe your boyfriend could be so insensitive. Jenna likes that, someone can finally understand me. Tony Brings Jenna into his office to discuss the paperwork for her new car and maybe some other things.

Jimmy's sale to the Indians is finished and they have left with the new car But not before Enieda whispers that she would like to put him under some either. Tacky is giving Jimmy a pat on the back for his good job. As their talking they are surprised by Dominick Dupree. Hey grandpa what are you doing here.

Hi Jimmy how's my little grandson. Grandpa I'm not that little boy anymore. Jimmy, I remember changing your diaper, you had the worst smelling shit in the world. You don't know how many times I barfed all over your changing table. Any way I'm meeting an old friend Dale McDonough, he called and said he wants to trade in his car for something a little sportier. Grandpa that guy has got to be in his early eighties like you. Why would he want a sportier car, they don't make them wheel chair accessible. Jimmy you little shit I'm in my eighties and I don't need a wheelchair. I'm sorry grandpa I was only teasing. By the way Jimmy is that girl in Tony's office wearing black wool underwear. Everyone turns to look at Tony's office than shakes their heads.

16 CHAPTER

The Old Man and Jimmy's Ride

Dominick Dupree started out as the son of Paul Dupree and Tillie Sorrono. Dominick left school at the age of fifteen to work for His uncle Salvatore Sorrono. Sal as everyone called him, sold produce to the many small Italian stores and restaurants. Sal had a horse drawn wagon that he used. The Korean War was going on and new trucks were in short supply. Sal needed a truck but couldn't afford the high price dealers wanted to charge. Dominick went to a dealer and the owner laughed at him, stating if you want a truck you have to pay the inflated price like everyone else. Dominick would not be put off, he went to the mayor's office and talked to one of his aides. He got a letter explaining that the mayor wants the dealer to sell to Salvatore any truck that he needs at cost or the city would investigate allegations the dealer was overcharging on new car sales. Dominick told the dealer that he shouldn't laugh at him because of his age. The dealer's daughter who worked in the office was impressed by Dominick and thought he was cute. Her father was also impressed and offered Dominick a job. Eventually Dominick married the owner's daughter and bought him out.

Dom looks out on the lot and see's Dale pull up in a car that Dom sold him just a year ago. Dale gets out of the driver's side and the right door opens to reveal a pair of long sexy legs with a short skirt. The women that emerges is tall, blond and quite sexy. Hmmm, is all Dom can say as the pair walk into the showroom. Hey Dale how's everything going, you look great as he grabs Dale's hand and shakes it. I wish I felt as good as you say I look. By the way this is my friend Sandra Kowalski. I met her when I took a trip to Europe last year.

Dom looks at Sandra and thinks I know why Dale doesn't feel good. We began writing to each other and I brought her over several months ago, to help me around the house, after Louise died. Dom extends his hand to Sandra and says I'm very happy to meet you I'm Dominick, Dale's friend from years ago. I'm glad to meet you Dominick and please say to me Sandy I like that better. Dom looks at Dale and says "say to me Sandy". Sorry Dom she doesn't quite have a good feel for the English language. Jimmy is standing there just listening to the conversation when Dominick hands him the keys to Dale's car. Jimmy go drive Dale's car and tell me if it's in good condition. You should learn how to appraise trade ins. Ok grandpa as he heads for the door. Sandy looks at Dale, I think I should go and make sure he doesn't try to break something on the car.

Without waiting for an answer Sandy bolts out the door to catch up with Jimmy. Jimmy gets in the driver's side and Sandy jumps in the right side. Sandy what are you doing, I'm just going to test drive the car to make sure there are no problems. I think you cute says Sandy so we have sex when we leave dealer. With that Sandy hitches herself up and pulls off her panties. Oh my god thinks Jimmy. He spots a pair of sunglasses on the dash so he puts them on so no one will identify him. Sandy kneels down on the front seat facing Jimmy, reaches around him and pulls the lever for tilt on the steering wheel. Jimmy I love tilt, much head room. Jimmy you are going to love this, in Poland I could suck down twenty weinies. Sandy I didn't know they had hot dog eating contests. Jimmy what's a hot dog eating contest. With that she attacks Jimmy's midsection. As their rolling along they come alongside a plumbing contractor's truck, with two Irish plumbers in the cab Sean and Patrick. Sean looks over and see's Sandy's rear end up in the air with no pants on. Damn Patrick will you look at that. Holy cow Sean I haven't seen a moon like that since I left Dublin. That's one beautiful moon, but Sean you're losing them. I can't help it Patrick there's a car in front with two old bags driving. Sean just honk the horn, maybe they'll move out of the way. Sean is laying on the horn to get the other car moving. The car in front has Ester and Mable. Ester is driving and Mable hears the honking. Ester what is that honking about?

Ester is looking in the rear view mirror and see's Sean and Patrick waving for the girls to move over. Mable there's two guys in this truck behind me and their waving for me to get out of their way. Screw them retorts Mable just give them the bird, they can go screw themselves. Ester rolls down the window and flips them the bird. Sean see's the bird, goes ballistic and floors the truck. He begins pushing the girls down the street. Both Ester and Mable are screaming at the top of their lungs, thinking they're going to die. At the last minute Ester does a high speed turn on two wheels and comes to rest at a restaurant. Mable calmly asks Ester if she really flipped them the bird. Ester nods yes and Mable screams you bitch are you trying to kill me. Jimmy is having the time of his life. I love the car business if this is the way it's always going to be.

Hey Sandy can you hum the eighteen twelve overture. Sandy nods yes and begins humming. Their coming up to a stop ahead sign and Jimmy thinks no way. They eventually end up in a shopping center way out in the parking lot. Sandy sits up and tells Jimmy. Now Jimmy it's your turn. With that she leans back, puts her legs up, grabs Jimmy's head and pulls it between her legs. Moments later all you can hear is steel bending and glass cracking with the sounds of Sandy moaning. After several minutes Jimmy comes up for air. The sunglasses are bent and the glass is cracked. Sandy what a pair of thighs. Jimmy I use the nutcracker thigh machine Dale just loves it.

Meanwhile Sean and Patrick having lost Jimmy are still talking about the great moon they saw. Sean says lets go to McKeevers bar for a pint and after we tell the gang maybe someone will buy us a drink. Patrick laughs those cheap lackeys won't buy us a drink. Sean maybe McKeever will pop for a pint. Patrick, McKeever is the cheapest of them all. Finally Jimmy and Sandy get back to the dealership. Jimmy comes in and hands the keys to Dominick. Grandpa that car is brand new, I don't think it's even broken in. Jimmy let me handle this, and he turns to Dale. Dale the kid says the car is a piece of shit. You haven't taken care of it. Dale looks amazed, Sandy is always taking it to one of those oil changing places. Sandy looks up in the air and starts to blush. Dale wonders maybe Sandy is changing someone else's oil. Dominick pats Dale on the back, don't worry Dale I'll give you a good deal. Why don't you two go into Rick Dixon's office to start the paperwork and I'll bring in the figures. Tricky introduces himself to Dale and Sandy. Tell me Dale is this car for you or this lovely lady. I could put it in both your names. Sandy leans over and puts her arm around Dale. Dale darling I would like it if the car was just in my name, because if something happened to you I would have it to remember you. Tricky questions Dale is that all right with you. Go ahead put it in her name only. Sandy Grabs Dale and plants a passionate kiss on him.

Dale tonight I am going to give you something very special. Dale thinks, oh God I hope my pacemaker can handle this. Do I have enough Viagra, I might be dead by morning. Tricky turns the paperwork around for Dale to look over. Dale check the figures and then sign where I have marked with an ex. Dale reaches into his vest pocket. I have to get out my cheaters, so I can see the figures. Dale pulls out a pair of glasses that the frames are all bent and the glass is taped together. Tricky is surprised by the glasses, Dale what happened to your glasses. Oh hell they just break. Well Dale why don't you buy a pair of new ones. Hell Mr. Dixon I buy a new pair every week. Nick has heard that the girl in Tony's Office has no pants on, so he gets a mop and bucket and starts washing the floor just outside Tony's office. He's bent down pretending to scrape something off the floor to try to get a better view, when Jenna spots him she smiles. What's your name cutie? Hey beautiful the names Nick. Well Nick if you got a couple of hundred maybe you could see what's causing your pants to suddenly bulge out. Jenna lightly kisses Nick, come down to the Kitty Litter Lounge and bring that money with you. The Girls and I will show you how to get rid of it.

17 CHAPTER

Nigel Noc-Noc Nelson

Dan goes to the customer lounge and gets a cup of coffee. When he sets it on his desk it suddenly begins to make small swirls, the swirls are getting more agitated then the pencil begins to vibrate. Oh shit he hollers stay away from the windows and overhead lights. Just then into the service doorway appears a Land Cruiser 5000, completely tricked out and jacked up. The audio system is turned all the way up. A couple of mercury vapor lights explode and a trouble lamp explodes. Dan goes over to the SUV, raps on the window and hollers turn off the audio. The audio is so loud Dan wonders how can the paint stays on the SUV with the way the panels are vibrating. The window rolls down and Nigel-Noc-Noc Nelson a local radio station DJ, says something to Dan although Dan can't hear what he's saying because the audio is so loud. Finally Dan screams shut off the Damn Radio. Nigel shuts it off and tells Dan, you don't have to scream I could hear you. Sorry Nigel you know I can't stand that rap music. What brings you in today? Dan I continually hear chimes or ringing coming from the front seats, and it's driving me crazy. Could you check into this and while it's here change the oil and rotate the tires. Nigel how often do you hear this. Dan I hear it all the time even with the radio on. Dan walks back to the service counter to write up the order and thinks how does this man hear anything.

Brian Moran walks into the showroom and approaches Al Farina, Tony's brother. Hi I'm looking for a new car. Al looks at Brian and says Listen kid maybe you should go and get one of those skate boards. Hey I just turned eighteen, my father said he was going to co-sign for a new car for me, but he really pissed me off because he backed out on his promise. I heard that Dominick's has a no money down deal going on, and I want in. Al kind of snickers, all right kid what's your name. I'm sorry it's Brian Moran. Listen Brian do you have a job? I work at the Duds & Suds. Al thinks for a moment. I might be able to put you in a slightly used convertible that we just took in. It was driven by an exotic dancer, would you be interested in something like that. Brian say's wow I would really like a convert so I could pick up beautiful girls.

Al Think's with a face like that the only thing you could pick up is a jar of acne cream. Just then Tony comes walking past Brian and Al. Al points out that's the girl who drove the convert. I hear she doesn't wear panties. Brian's excited I would really like to see the car and maybe I could smell it, oops I mean drive it. Brian watches Jenna walk away and just pictures her on his lap in that car. Ok Brian here's the price of the car, is this too much for you to pay? I don't know if I can afford the car. Do you think I could pick up girls driving that car. Now listen kid what you need to do is go out and get a nice white pull over, tan jeans, a gold necklace and a fake gold watch. Than you go to the high school soccer field and drop the top and sit up on the front seat. When the girls see you they will come running because they will think your rich. Especially the blonds. Brian says I don't care what it costs, as he is thinking about the soccer field.

18 CHAPTER

Jimmy and The Nun

Jimmy's hanging out in the showroom when in walks a nun from St Sylvester Parish. Jimmy recognizes her from when he was in grammar school. Hello Sister Mary how are you. Oh hello Melvin how are you? Sister Mary it's Jimmy I was in your fifth grade. You're thinking about my dad. Oh Jimmy, in that sweet Irish accent, you look just like your father. Sister Mary how can I help you? I came in to buy a new car for the convent. I have a specification sheet on what we want on the new car. All the nuns voted on what we want. Jimmy takes the sheet from Sister Mary and looks it over.

Sister it says here that you want a new econo fifty wagon with a five hundred watt sound system, ten disc CD changer, and the four hundred horsepower turbo V8. Sister why do you want the sound system. Jimmy we need it to blow off those rappers who play that disgusting horrible crap they call music. I especially like playing Handles Messiah and blow the windows out of their cars. I understand sister, but why the big engine. Jimmy on Saturday night we have drag races, and I want to beat that St Margaret's convent they have a fully blown sixty three Camaro and I want to blow them away. Sister Mary I put together the invoice price of the car you want.

Now I want you to understand this is the price that we pay for the car. I'm not making a nickel on this sale. The price is seventeen thousand four hundred sixty dollars. Jimmy's smiling because no one can really beat his price. Suddenly Sister Mary smacks him on his hands with a ruler. Listen you little turd the Jew down the street gave me a price about two grand cheaper. Jimmy's rubbing his hand and says to Sister Mary I'm selling you this car at invoice. Don't give that crap if the Jew can sell me the car two grand cheaper, you can't be telling me the truth. Sister Mary smacks him again. Jimmy if you don't give me a better deal I'm going to tell what I saw you doing with Blackly Sullivan in the coat room. Sister I was only seven at the time, and we were only experimenting at the time. Jimmy I'll tell them you were thirteen and had your pants down.

Jimmy is panicky, Sister hold on for just a second I need to see my dad. Jimmy rushes into Tacky's office. Dad Sister Mary is in the showroom and she wants me to sell her a car two thousand under invoice or she's going to tell everyone about something's I did in grammar school. Tacky laughs Jimmy don't worry she did the same thing to me when I was in her class. In fact she uses this whenever she needs something. She's done this to all the stores in town. Jimmy just send her in and I will get this worked out. Jimmy brings Sister Mary into Tacky's office. Tacky smiles, hello Sister Mary I can't believe you're still alive, you got to be about a hundred. Sister Mary raises her ruler at Tacky, Listen you old turd I want this car at a better price than the Jew down the street. Sister I'll sell you the car at whatever the price you want, because I can always claim I was giving to charity. On second thought I'll give you the car for free if you hold an event that features my dealership. Sister Mary comes over by Tacky grabs him by his ear, Melvin I never thought you would turn out as nice as you are. The sisters will say a prayer for you.

19 CHAPTER

The Doctor

Faruk is pacing the showroom, the traffic has not been very good, when a distinguished black gentleman comes walking in. Faruk approaches the gentleman and introduces himself. Hi I'm Faruk Maroqus, as he's extending his hand he slightly bows and clicks his heels together. Hello Dr. D Malcolm Jones here and I want some information on your top of the line vehicles. Dr. Jones nice meeting you, come on and I will show you some of our top of the line cars. He brings the doctor over to the Sentinel 455 and goes over all the standard equipment available on the sedans and on the convertibles.

Dr. Jones is impressed with Faruk. He liked the continental flair and Faruk's knowledge of the cars. After viewing several sedans the doctor settles on a two door completely loaded. They test drive the car and as the doctor is driving, Faruk is pointing out some good handling characteristics. When they get back to Faruk's office they agree on a price. The doctor is really happy with the buying process. As their taking the paperwork to Tricky's office the doctor complements Faruk. I have purchased many cars but this is the first time, I have enjoyed the experience. Thank you so much Faruk. Faruk introduces Dr. Jones to Tricky and the doctor fills out a credit app. Tricky runs a credit bureau on the doctor and a lot of Jones come up with bad credit. I'm sorry doctor I need more information D Malcolm Jones is not enough I need the first full name instead of just an initial. Dr. Jones replies I don't want to use my first name because it's embarrassing. Listen doctor I will not disclose your name to anyone or put it on the paperwork. I just need it for the credit bureau. Dr. begins to get red in his face, ok my first name is Defecation. Tricky's teeth almost fall out of his mouth, did I hear you right, you said Defecation. That's right, that's my first name. Holy shit doc how did you get a name like that? The doctor begins his story.

My mother was born down in Alabama. She came up to Chicago when she was about ten. Both my grandparents were killed in a car accident, and she was sent to live in a foster home. The people she lived with wouldn't send her to school and made her work cleaning people's houses. She wound up getting pregnant by a gang banger. They were living in the projects and when she was about to deliver me they called an ambulance to take me to Cook County Hospital. While they were driving I was delivered in the ambulance. The paramedics laid me on her stomach, and I pooped. The girl said oh look defecation. My mother who was not literate said oh my goodness that's such a strong name. I think I'll name him that. The one paramedic said that sure is strong. That's how I got my name.

Those people could have told my mother what that really meant, but they didn't they just kept laughing, every time she said it again. Listen Doc why don't you just change it. It's an easy thing to do. The doctor say's I thought about it a lot, but I feel I would be doing a disservice to my mother. I feel a great honor having overcome aversion to become a doctor. Ok doc I'll put in your corrected data. The bureau says you look good, no shitty credit. Oops sorry just a Freudian slip, lets get everything printed out and signed so you can drive home that new car. Faruk was just outside Tricky's office and heard the story about the good doctors name. He walks back to the wash rack to see how their cleaning up the doctors car' Charlie is going over the car to make sure everything perfectly clean. Faruk approaches him and tells him about the doctors real name.

Charlie drives the car around to the side door of the showroom and gives the keys to Faruk, to go over everything and make sure he's happy. Dr. Jones comes out and gets in the car with Faruk. They go over all options and warranty specifications. Finally Faruk tells the doctor you will get a form in the mail that asks for your opinion of our dealership. The doctor smiles don't worry I won't give you a shitty report. Ok doc no defecation, I appreciate that, and gets out of the car. Charlie overhears what Faruk just said and with the pained look that he sees on the doctors face smiles. Faruk I think you just blew it with that last remark. Faruk laughs I couldn't help it that just came out.

Noc-Noc & Penny

Several mechanics are looking over Noc-Noc's SUV trying to find the noise that Noc-Noc is complaining about. Their testing all the various warning systems and cannot find anything wrong. Luther the used car mechanic comes walking by and the guys tell him about the ringing noise. Luther goes into the customer lounge and asks Noc-Noc about the noise He tells Luther that it doesn't happen all the time and sometimes the Suv isn't even running. Luther smiles I think I can solve your problem. He walks out to the SUV opens the door and starts searching around the front seats. After several minutes he finds what he was looking for and returns to the customer lounge. Here idiot here's your noise you were complaining about and hands Noc-Noc a cellphone. Oh shit I wondered what happened to that. Luther goes back to the techs. Who were looking for the problem? That idiot left his cell phone jammed in between the seats, so tell Dan to charge him the idiot charge.

Tacky's secretary is Penny as mentioned earlier. Every day at exactly twelve she walks through the service dept. Penny is built like an amazon women. She is perfect with great long legs that are always shown off by a mini skirt. Rick and Ron have always fantasized about what she has on under her skirt. Does she have panties on, and maybe they are see through, or does she dress au- natural. The boys have this ritual that when she comes through the service dept. they pretend to be looking under a vehicle in the path of her route. Today as usual when she enters the service area the radio station begins playing a Bob Segar song called the strut. Both guys are crawling under the car to get as good a view as possible. As she's walking past she begins to fumble in her purse, and she drops her keys. As if in slow motion she starts to lean over to pick up her keys.

Both guys look as her skirt slowly begins to slide up on her thy. They can't believe this, they will solve the bet. All of a sudden Whinnying Willie pulls a car out of a bay and cuts off their view. Hey Guys I'm going to Carols Chicken Shack to pick up some lunch, do you guys want anything. Both Ron and Rick jump up and grab Willie out of the car. Willie were going to kill you. Charlie jumps in and separates the guys. Fellas there's always tomorrow. Willie is complaining, if they don't want chicken than just say so. Afterword's Rick says to Ron, you know every time she walks through the service dept. that same song plays. Ron who is brain dead about anything other than cars says you know I think your right.

Tony's sitting in his office thinking about visiting the Kitty Litter Lounge, when a raving maniac comes running into the showroom wanting to see whoever sold him the car. Mike slides under his desk to hide. Tony comes out of his office and confronts Sam Britton who recently purchased a new car from Dominick's. Tony shouts, quit screaming what's the problem. Sam screams I purchased this car and I was promised the payment would not exceed two hundred a month for forty eight months. Now I received a payment book for two hundred a month for sixty months. Listen Sam let me check this out and I think we can get it worked out for you. Tony goes to see Tricky and find out why Sam Britton has sixty payments. Tricky starts laughing,

Tony don't you remember, we quoted him two hundred a month for the balance after his down payment. If I remember right his wife didn't want the three thousand down payment to get to that two hundred payment. Besides she wanted that exclusive extended warranty that cost another three grand. Ok Tricky I'll handle this. Tony goes back to Sam and asks Sam can I see the payment book. Sam gives the book to Tony who proceeds to rip out the last two years of payments' Sorry Sam they gave you someone else's payment book. Sam apologizes, Tony I'm sorry I know you guys would never try to cheat someone.

21 CHAPTER

The Twins

Elk is wandering around the showroom when he spots an SUV pulling up with a middle age women driving and two girls sitting in the back. As they walk into the showroom, Elk extends his hand and says I'm Eldon Kendale but everyone calls me Elk. The woman smiles and says that's a cute name, my name is Bambi Bristol and these are my twin daughters Cindy and Mindy they came to help me pick out a new car. Elk smiles so you're picking out a car for the girls. Oh no Elk I'm need a new car for myself. Elk is puzzled and says who owns the new SUV. Elk the SUV belongs to the girls.

They work really hard all the time and make a lot of money. Elk is staring at the girls as their sucking on lolly pops. Elk you wouldn't believe the money they make. Just last week they went over to a neighbor's house who is a widower. They mowed his lawn and cleaned his yard. I think they also cleaned his house. They were in there for a long time and made three hundred bucks each. He would like them to come over at least every week. The girls smile at Elk and keep sucking on their lolly pops. Elk turns to Bambi your girls really like those lolly pops. Bambi smiles you know Elk they have always liked sucking on something. I had a terrible time trying to stop them from sucking on their thumbs. Elk's mind goes into hyper drive, as he imagines what he would like to do with the girls. Tell me Bambi what car are you interested in. Elk I don't have a lot of money so I would like to test drive the Econo thirty.

Elk moans that car is the hardest for him to get into. Elk goes out to the new car lot and picks out an Econo thirty that he thinks Bambi would like. He pulls it up by the showroom door and escorts Bambi and the girls to the car. Bambi is overjoyed Elk has pulled up her favorite color Seafoam Green. Elk how did you know that is my favorite color. Elk Smiles I think it matches your personality. Bambi gets in the driver's seat, the girls get in the back and Elk squeezes himself into the passenger seat. Bambi tells Elk I'm happy were driving this car, but I really want to go several different dealers to get the best price. Elk thinks oh shit I've got another one of them.

Well Bambi I think it's a good idea to make sure you get the best price and the best service, wherever you buy this car. Elk is trying to turn and position himself so he's facing Bambi as she's driving. He's having a really hard time but finally gets turned around. Elk is telling Bambi about all the great features about the car when he glances into the rear seat. Cindy is sliding the lolly pop in and out of her mouth and is slowly pulling up her skirt. Elk looks at Mindy and she is doing the same thing. Elk begins to perspire profusely. Bambi see's this happening and tells Elk I'm sorry Elk I should have turned on the AC, I didn't think it was so hot in here.

The girls have him really going as their rubbing themselves under their skirts. Elk keeps trying to concentrate on Bambi and the test drive. When they get back to the dealership Elk escorts Bambi to the service dept. Bambi I want you to meet Dan the service manager. Dan extends his hand and says I hope we will see you again because we have an award winning service dept. Bambi's impressed no one ever took her seriously. Finally they go to Elks office and negotiate a selling price. Again Bambi is impressed, Elk is not trying to push her into the sale but asks her about her job and interests.

Bambi smiles, Elk I like you, and I like the price. Why don't we write it up on the car I test drove. Elk shakes her hand I'm sure you will love this car and our dealership. Elk takes her to Tricky's office and introduces her. He gives Tricky the paper work and says I'm going to run it through the car wash to freshen it up. Both girls beg Bambi to ride with Elk through the wash. Elk gets in the driver's seat and both girls get in the back seat. Charlie watches Elk drive into the wash thinking how does he fit in that car. Several minutes pass and as the car emerges Elk is in the back seat and both girls are in the front. Charlie does a double take. Elk couldn't turn around in a closet how the hell did he get into the back seat. The girls pull the car up to the front of the building. Elk squeezes himself out of the car. Charlie sees him reach into his pocket, pull out a bunch of bills and give them to the girls. The twins reach up and give Elk a kiss on his cheek.

22 CHAPTER

Larry Doyle or L D

Mike hasn't had a good up today as they call it in the car business. He's getting worried, Tacky gets uptight when someone doesn't have at least one sale or a good prospect every day. About this time a man and a women come through the door, just as Mike is walking that way. Hi I'm Mike Stevens and what can I do for you. The man holds out his hand. Hi I'm Lawrence J. Doyle and this is the little woman, but you can call me Larry. A lot of my friends call me L.D. Mike smiles, what can I do for you L.D. Well Mike I'm looking for a car for the little woman and I would like a price on the Sentinel 455. Mike I want to warn you, I won't pay full price unless you throw in floor mats.

Mike is getting weak knees' and almost passes out. He thinks I can't believe this, there really is a car god. Mike shakes Larry's hand and leads them into his office and says I think we can work it out. Larry turns to his wife, see honey this is how you buy a new car. Mike begins to write up the new car. As he turns the sales agreement around he motions to Larry that he has included the premium floor mats. Listen Larry because you're such a serious shopper I have included Dominick's email address to be put on your rear window, and pin striping at no extra cost. Larry nudges his wife. See honey this is how you negotiate. Mike I have to inquire, I have heard the environmental protection package can cost up to several thousand dollars. Mike replies L.D. just for you I'm only going to charge twelve hundred.

Larry shakes his hand, sounds good to me. Larry's wife pipes up, Larry there's a sign on the wall that it's only two hundred and forty nine dollars. Mike quickly counters by saying, Larry that's the down payment. Larry is there anything else you might want on the new car. Larry starts thinking, Mike breaks in, Larry how about an extended warranty. Larry flashes a wide grin, Mike you took the words right out of my mouth. Ok Larry how about four years fifty thousand miles, for only eight hundred dollars. Larry thinks that's great, but his wife screams, Larry the car has a three year thirty six thousand mile factory warranty. I know sweetie but you can never have too much insurance.

His wife turns to Mike can I get an insurance policy on Larry that if he dies the car will be paid off. Mike adds, of course we can include this in the payments. Ok put it in the payments he may not make it home. Larry what color do you want. Mike the car is for the little woman she should pick out the color. Mike turns to Larry's wife what color would you like. She responds, can I get it in effin purple. Mike frowns, we don't have that color. She responds how about dark red because that's the way I feel. Mike leads them to Tricky's office, hoping the monthly payment won't blow them out of the box. Tricky runs a bureau on them and gives Mike the thumbs up. Mike thinks, Tacky gives a bonus for the highest gross profit on a single sale and he thinks he's got it locked up.

Jimmy, Felix & Elvis

Jimmy's pacing the showroom, pumped up from his earlier sale to the Indian family. A Lincoln pulls up by the showroom and a short black man emerges. Jimmy thinks this is my next customer, and as he comes through the showroom door, Jimmy sticks out his hand and says hi I'm Jimmy what can I do for you. The Black guy looks at Jimmy with distain and says are they hiring school kids as greeters. Jimmy takes this as an affront, Listen I'm Jimmy Dupree, who the hell are you. Felix slams on the brakes, turns to Jimmy and says who did you say you are? I'm Jimmy Dupree, my dad is Tacky Dupree. Tony see's this happening and intercedes. Jimmy this is Felix Washington he's another sales person for Dupree. Felix smiles sorry I didn't think there were so many Dupree's. Jimmy sticks out his hand, hey nice to meet you but you're so short how do you make any sales. Felix laughs, actually my size is an advantage, and you will see me working my magic later. Listen Tony I took that Lincoln to my cousin's place in Indiana. He really liked the car, but on the way back it broke down. If it wasn't for the help I probably wouldn't have been able to get here. Tony asks who was your helper. Felix replies Hoosier Helper. Tony is perplexed Who's your helper. Felix replies I told you Hoosier Helper. Tony throws up his hands, all I asked is who's your helper. Felix replies you idiot it's Hoosier Helper. Tony walks away, this guy is an idiot.

Jimmy and Tim are sitting at Tim's desk. Jimmy asks Tim, hey you want to smoke a dooby. I have some grass hidden in my shoe. Tim thinks this is a good idea. Jimmy comes back I don't have any papers, no problem Jimmy I got a ton of them. A lot of cars that get traded in have a stash of grass or shorts in the ash trays. As their heading out through the service dept. Jimmy spots a guy He's never seen before. Tim who is that guy? Tim answers oh that's Glen he cleans up all the used cars. Jimmy can't take his eyes off him he has a pure white set of coveralls with red piping going down both sides. The large G is monogramed on the back of his coveralls in sequins and on the front he has the name Glen stitched on his top pocket. What is driving Jimmy crazy is his outfit is immaculate.

Tim how does he keep that outfit so clean. Tim Smiles, he takes great pride in his coveralls. Jimmy says great pride, are you crazy, there isn't a mark of dirt anywhere. Jimmy can't stop staring at this guy, not only is his outfit perfect but he has pork chop side burns and his hair is combed to perfection. As they pass Jimmy hears him singing softly, and take a walk down lonely street to heart break hotel. Jimmy says he sounds just like Elvis. Glen looks up, excuse me son did I hear you mention Elvis. Tim cuts in, Glen this is Jimmy Dupree, Tacky's son. I'm sorry Jimmy I didn't mean no disrespect by calling you son. Jimmy sticks out his hand to Glen and says, no problem Glen. You know you sound just like Elvis. Everyone tells me I sound just like him.

He was a great man and a legend. Say are you guys going out for something to eat, and if so could you bring me back a couple of jelly donuts. No Glen were going out back and smoke a little weed. Glen suddenly has a troubled look on his face, as he slowly shakes his head. You boys don't know what that can do to you. Look what it did to me. Excuse me I meant Elvis. Jimmy is walking away and still looking back at Glen. Tim how long has Glen been working here. Tim scratches his head if I recall he applied for a job around August of seventy seven. Tacky said he looked like hell, but convinced Tacky he could do the job because he was an old country boy and loved to play gospel tunes on his guitar. Hell Jimmy if you think his coveralls are neat you should see him at our Christmas parties. The outfits he wears will blow you away, and the way he plays those Elvis songs with all those gyrations, the girls all wet their pants. As Jimmy's lighting up a joint he tells Tim if I remember right my mom told me that Elvis died back in seventy seven.

Maybe that's really Elvis. Tim starts to laugh, come on Jimmy why would he be working here. Come to think of it Tacky tells me he rarely cashes his pay check, and seems to disappear on weekends. They finally get Jimmy's demo towed in from the police pond, and of course the wheels, tires and radio are missing. The front is still covered with road tar. Tacky walks around the car shaking his head. He thinks I should just kill that kid. Tacky calls over Willie the new car porter who cleans all the new cars when they are transported in. Willie get the shit cleaned off this car. I'm going to order new wheels and tires. Hell Tacky moans Willie How am I going to get all this tar off the front. Willie quit whining just use the steam cleaner to blow it off, but don't get it on yourself, your black enough. I don't want the NAACP coming down on me. Tacky goes over to the parts counter. Wesley get new wheels and tires for that demo and get the primo sound system. No problem Tacky I'll make sure we get it ASAP.

Hey Tacky maybe you should fire Jimmy, He's always causing you problems. You know what Wes maybe you're right I'll fire him and then I'll fire you for all the problems you cause. Oh Tacky I'm only kidding, can't you take a joke. Right now Wes I'm not in the mood for jokes, he turns and walks away. Ziggy smiles Wes I don't think you should mess with that order. Wes tries to smile but nods in agreement with Ziggy.

Herb, Martha & The Roof

Felix is still a little ticked off over being stranded in Indiana, when in walks a couple. Herb and Martha have spent the last several days touring every dealer in town to try and get the best deal. Felix approaches Herb, puts out his hand and says welcome to Dupree's where you always get the best deal. I'm Felix and I want this to be good experience for you. Herb introduces himself and his wife Martha. Excuse me what did you say your name was. Felix smiles and introduces himself again. Felix we are looking for a fully loaded Econo 50 four door. We're going to trade in our car and we want your best price. We have gone to several dealers and would like to see how you stack up. Felix walks them over to an Econo 50 that's on the showroom floor. I stack up a little over five feet, but this is the price of the Econo 50. Martha doesn't like the way Felix is talking to them. Herb maybe we should just go back to that other dealer and buy the car. Listen says Felix I know you really don't want to buy the car from me. Maybe because I'm a short black man. I think Martha wants to go back to that dealer and talk to that young blond salesman. I think I can really get you a better deal. Besides we have the exact car in stock. Herb turns to Martha, listen maybe we should see what Felix has to offer. Felix smiles he has leveled the playing field. Ok folks I need to appraise your trade so I can give you an accurate price. Felix calls Tony to his office. He gives the keys to Tony. Hey Tony get me the best trade in price for these wonderful couple. Tony comes back and gives Felix the sheet that tells him what is wrong with the trade in and what is the value. Felix starts writing down figures and turns the sheet around for Herb and Martha to view. Martha frowns this is exactly the same price we got from another dealer. Hold on says Felix let me talk to my manager and see if we can make this deal sweeter. Felix goes to Tony's office, hey listen can we put a little more into the trade to make this deal. Tony shakes his head, I heard that they went to all the dealers and I stretched on this deal, so I hope you could put something together. Felix goes back to his office. I'm sorry folks the only thing I can do is to offer free floor mats and a free oil change. Martha chimes up just give us the keys to our car so we can leave. Felix says I gave the keys to Herb. Herb goes I didn't get any keys. Felix comes back I'm sure I gave you the keys. Herb is searching his pockets. I can't find the keys. Meanwhile Tacky is walking through the showroom when he gets water dripping from the ceiling on to his head. What the hell it's not even raining outside, and the ceiling is leaking.

Tacky goes into his office and tells his secretary Penny I just had a roof put on two years ago, call the roofer and the HVAC contractor to find out what the hell is going on. He calls Charlie to get up to the showroom and get this cleaned up. Back in Felix's office, Felix swears he gave the keys to Herb. Listen folks I believe we are the best dealer that you could buy a car from. We have an award winning service dept. Also I see that you don't live that far away from us. Herb looks at Martha I think he has a good point. What the hell let's just buy the car here. Meanwhile Lars Niemann the roofer walks into the showroom and goes to Tacky's office. What are you calling about, I replaced your roof a couple of years ago, it should be good for several years more. Tacky escorts him to the showroom where the leak is coming through the ceiling. Lars says it's not raining so why is this my problem. Tacky who has not had a good day so far, retorts I don't know where it's coming from, if it comes through the ceiling, it, s your problem. Lars gets out his ladder and climbs to the roof. Several minutes later he climbs down with a hand full of keys. Tacky is this the area where the appraised trades are parked. Tacky says yes why do you ask? Lars hands him a handful of keys. These are only a small amount of what's on the roof. There has to be several hundred pounds of keys up there, and they punctured the roof. Now the water from the AC is leaking through the roof. Tacky frowns and shaking his head tells Lars, clean up the roof and repair it.

25 CHAPTER

Mike's Gas

Mikes Diarrhea has finally subsided and turned into gas big time his office smells worse than a sewage retention pond. Emil and his wife Georgann are approaching Dupree's looking for a new car. Georgann is giving Emil a hard time reminding him he always gives in to any salesperson regardless of what their buying. Ok Georgann I will be a good boy and not say anything. You can do all the negotiating, and promptly rips off a major fart. God Emil you're so gross, can't you control yourself. I'm going to be so embarrassed if you do that in front of the salesman. Mike's in his office waving his arms, trying to get rid of the smell. Emil see's Mike waving and thinks he's waving to them. Emil approaches Mike and says I saw you waving at us, do we know you. Mike always fast on his feet responds I think I sold you your last car. Georgann replies no we have never purchased a car from you or your dealership. Mike responds maybe it was a daytime drama, that I was watching and you were the heroine. Georgann blushes slightly and replies, I do think I look just like Miraball. Mike smiles and thinks a good line will almost always turn into a sale.

Mike reaches out to shake Emil's hand and as Emil reaches over to shake Mike's hand he rips off a really loud one. Mike in turn, even though he's trying to hold it back, rips off another loud one. Emil starts to laugh, see honey I'm not the only one that's in harmony with nature. Mike reaches for Georgann's hand. I don't know if I want to shake hands if that's what is going to happen. Mike apologizes and tells Georgann it was a freak of nature. As they walk into Mikes office Emil rips of another one. Mike thinks thank god he's got me covered. Georgann gasps, Emil that one is the worse one ever. Mike smiles oh yes. Now my lovely lady what brings you to Dupree's? This is my husband Emil and I'm Georgann, were looking at the new Sentinel 455 four door sedan. I'm sorry I forgot to introduce myself my name is Mike Stevens. Emil reaches out for Mikes hand again, But Mike pulls back. We're not going to do that again. Georgann laughs thank god I've had about as much as I can handle. Before we get down to working out all the details and options, why don't we drive one. Mike states I have a convertible parked right outside.

Why don't we drive that one? Emil resists we don't want a convert we want a sedan. Mike comes back they all drive the same and besides I would have to clean up a sedan so you could drive it. Georgann looks at Emil what's the difference lets drive it. Instinctively Georgann gets behind the wheel, Mike gets in the passenger seat and Emil gets in the back. When they pull away Georgann unties the ribbon on her pony tail, letting her hair blow in the wind. Mike thinks today is going to be my day for highest gross on deliveries, and maybe a hat trick because a convert has a higher gross profit than a sedan. Her skirt is blowing up slightly and a semi passes on the right, slows slightly, toots the horn and hollers, hey cutie. Mike can tell Georgann is really digging the attention. Emil crouches up close to the front seat and says Georgann what do you think of the ride. Emil I remember Timmy McCann's convert. We really had a good time. I lost my virginity on top of the back seat. Emil groans I didn't know that. Georgann responds you know I wasn't a virgin when I met you. Besides Timmy introduced us. Emil slumps back in the seat and Georgann has a smile on her face and a distant look in her eyes. When they get back to the showroom, Georgann as she is getting out runs her fingers over the finish of the car. Emil is protesting now can we concentrate on a sedan. Georgann gives Emil a cold stare I told you I was going to do the negotiating, and proceeds to walk in through the showroom door, leaving Mike and Emil standing by the car.

Mike feels bad for Emil so he lightens up the situation. Emil pull my finger, and Mike rips off a really loud one. Damn Emil I almost crapped in my pants. Emil Laughs ok Mike pull my finger. Emil rips a really gross one and they both laugh. When they get into Mikes office Mike asks Georgann is the convert going to be in your name or Emil's. Emil begins to object but Georgann cuts him off. Mike it's going in my name, but you can put Emil's name as secondary Mike rights it up at almost full list. Listen Georgann I think you're a lot younger than Emil so when you get into the finance office you might want to purchase an insurance policy on Emil. Mike you just read my mind I'm so happy that you are our salesman. Mike shakes hands with Emil and Georgann gives Mike a big hug.

26 CHAPTER

Brian, Max and Cool Ray

Brian Moran has gone home with his new convertible. He's going to change clothes and go to the soccer field that Tony told him where he could pick up girls. Brian pulls into the driveway at home and Jack comes out to see the car Brian just purchased. Brian how the hell could you afford this car. I told you dad Dupree's has a no money down offer. Damn Brian I can't believe you could get a car on the money you make. Dad listen it's not brand new, it was traded in by an exotic dancer. You know Brian, I think it belonged to Juicy Jenna. Dad how would you know it belonged to Juicy Jenna unless you went to the Kitty Litter Lounge. No Brian I saw her at the gas station several times, and they told me who it belonged to. Yea sure says Brian I'll bet that's not where you saw her. Brian changes clothes and sneaks into his dad's room to grab some bling to impress the girls. Several minutes later he pulls up to the soccer field, drops the top and sits up on top of the front seat, just like Tony told him. He's having a good time watching young girls getting all sweaty. Across the field Max the mauler pulls in. Max is the bouncer and part owner of the Kitty Litter Lounge. He likes to look at sweaty young girls and potential dancers at the club. As He's checking it out he sees his girlfriend's car, but there is a guy in the front seat. Max comes unglued, if she is cheating on me I'm going to kill her and that chicken neck driving her car.

Max walks over to Brian's car. Hi is this your car. Brian answers yes I just bought it from Dupree's. Max grabs him by his neck, who are you kidding chicken neck this is my girlfriend's car. Brian is chocking and gasps I just purchased this from Dupree's. Please believe me, I know that Jenna traded it in. Max not releasing his grip grabs his cell phone and speed dials Juicy Jenna. Jenna answers, Max is screaming at her, how could you trade in the car I gave to you. Jenna screams back, I know this car used to belong to your old girlfriend. Max still screaming tells Jenna I own that car. You better meet me at Dupree's so I can get this worked out. Max releases his grip on Brian and gets in the passenger's seat. Ok chicken neck you drive. Tony's standing in the showroom and see's Jenna pull up in her new convert. He's smiling as she approaches the door. Then see's Brian drive in with this huge ape in the passenger seat. All he can say is oh-oh. Jenna comes up to Tony and gives him a kiss on the cheek. Tony, Max will probably want me to give the car back, but I want you to help me keep it. Tony' got a real bad feeling, this may not turn out well. Max comes storming into the showroom. He looks at Tony, are you the person that sold my girlfriend that new car. Tony hesitates, not wanting to get knocked out.

Yes I sold her the car. Max growls, That's my car how could you take it in trade and sell her a car without a title from the trade in. Tony thinks fast did you give her the car. Max takes a step back. I gave her the car to use, not trade it in. Jenna pipes up, so Max you told me it was my car. If it was my car I should be able to do what I want with it. Besides that tramp that used to drive it probably had no pants on and stained the seat. She turns to Brian did you see the stain on the seat and smell it. I can't believe you would buy a car with that smell on the seat. Brian is shaking his head no but, his face is turning purple. Tony looks at Max, listen you gave her the car. If you make her give it back, you're going to regret it. About this time Felix hearing all the racket comes out of his office and looks over at Max. Max what the hell are you hollering about? Tony, thankful for the intervention, say Felix do you know him. Felix laughs this is my cousin on my mom's side. Can't you see the resemblance? Tony thinks Max is easily six foot five and three

63

hundred pounds and Felix barely is five foot tall. You know Felix I do see the resemblance. Ok Max what are you screaming about?

Max comes back listen Felix my girlfriend traded in the convert that I gave her, she doesn't have the title and my permission to trade it. Felix takes Jenna's hand and says my beautiful lady how could Max deny you having a new car. Jenna is so happy she gives Felix a big hug. Max come into my office I want to talk to you. Max follows Felix into his office and after several minutes Max comes out smiling. Ok Jenna you can keep the new car. Jenna is so happy she gives Max a real wet kiss and tells him not to go back to work, but to come over to her place and celebrate. Max turns to Brian, what were you doing at the soccer field? Brian tells him he was trying to pick up girls. Max tells Brian you're not going to pick up anyone unless you can flash some green. Listen Brian I am always looking for new girls at the club so I want you to get me some. Here's a thousand, just go back and flash it around. You should be able to get at least several blonds, to work it the club. Brian can't believe this, it's like a fantasy, gosh Mr. Max thanks a lot.

Back in the service department Dan notices that Cool Ray worked through lunch. Cool Ray comes up to Dan and says Dan listen I worked through lunch because I wanted to have lunch with my girlfriend. She gets off at about a little after one and we wanted to have lunch together. Dan not real happy with Ray shakes his head and tells Ray I'm not happy that you took upon yourself to change what time you're having lunch. Dan I'm really sorry that I didn't consult you before I did it. Ok Ray go and have lunch with your girlfriend but next time please ok it with me before you do something like that. Wow thanks Dan, Cool Ray bolts out the back door where there is a car waiting for him. They drive to the back of the lot, way in the corner. Dan turns to Matt, I guess they just want to visit while having lunch. Matt smiles, their going to have lunch, but the car will probably be rocking and rolling in a few minutes. Dan looks bewildered, why would it be rocking? Matt still smiling tells Dan you are a real piece of work.

27 CHAPTER

Clark Gas

After smoking a little weed with Jimmy, Tim gravitates to the customer lounge to watch TV, and get away from everyone. The news comes on and the announcer shows a clip of a Clark gas station that has just been robbed. Tim comments I think this is the fifth Clark station that's been robbed. The commentator reports that this is the fifth station that's been robbed. Tim is proud because he remembered that there have been five robberies of Clark gas stations. The station shows a composite drawing of the robber. Tim comments he looks a lot like the guy were trying to get financed on a new car. The service customer reacts, you don't sell cars to thieves do you. Tim laughs, hey we only sell cars to anyone who can afford it. We don't take large cash payments. Over the intercom Tim gets paged to the finance office. When he walks into the office Tricky says I got some good news and some bad news. Ok Tricky what's the good news? I finally got that guy financed, but the bad news is the finance company wants another thousand down. Tim remarks the guy were selling the car to looks just like the guy who's been robbing all the Clark gas stations. Maybe we should call the police, Tricky says just get the guy in here, and let's get the deal done. Tim goes back to his desk and pulls out the deal, gets on the phone and calls him. Hello Franklin this is Tim from Duprees we finally got an ok on the financing. Franklin gives a small cheer, that's great Tim, when can I come in to pick up the car. Well Franklin I have some bad news, the finance company wants another thousand down to do the deal. Ok Tim I can handle that. I'll bring in the thousand when I pick up the car. That's fantastic Franklin what time do you want to come in.

Hey Tim how late are the Clark stations open, and where is the closest Clark station to your dealership. Tim begins to stutter, I think there's a station just south of our location and its open all night. Hey Tim that's great see you in about an hour or so. Tim hurries back to the finance office. Oh my god Tricky you won't believe this, I called Franklin and told him about the extra thousand needed. He answered that it's no problem. So what are you so upset about Tim? Tricky you don't understand he wants to know where the closest Clark station is to the dealership. Maybe we should call the police and warn them that there could be another robbery. This guy has to be the robber. Tricky holds up his right hand to calm Tim. Calm down Tim, if this guy is the robber let's get the deal done, and then call the law. Don't you want to get paid your commission? Tim smiles, Tricky you are the best. I can't believe how you remain so cool, you are the kinkiest. Tim heads back to get the car cleaned up for delivery.

28 CHAPTER

Jimmy and The Farmer

Jimmy is chilling out in the showroom and spots a guy pulling up in an old beat up pickup truck. The man gets out and heads over to the most expensive vehicle in stock the land cruiser diamond edition. Jimmy starts to laugh. That guy probably couldn't buy one wheel off that land cruiser. What is also funny to Jimmy is the guy is dressed in bib overalls with a straw hay and old work boots. Jimmy thinks I think I'll have some fun with this guy, I'm not doing anything anyhow. Jimmy walks out and asks what he can do for this man. The man asks Jimmy how much can I buy this Vehicle for and can I test drive it. Jimmy puts his hand on the man's shoulder, I think you might be better off looking at our Econo fifty sedan or you could go down the street and check out some cheap cars at the Chevy dealer. Jimmy turns around and motions for the guy to follow him. As their walking into the showroom Jimmy is unaware that Tacky has been watching them. Jimmy walks over to a Econo 30 sedan. Sir I think this more for your liking. The customer shakes his head I asked for a price on that vehicle I was looking at. Tacky steps in, I'm sorry sir my name is Melvin Dupree Would you like to drive that land cruiser. Hi Mr. Dupree I would really like to drive it and maybe we could negotiate on a reasonable price. Tacky grabs Jimmy, get a dealer plate and the keys for that land cruiser, before I kill you.

Jimmy doesn't know what to say, so he gets the keys and a plate. Tacky tells Jimmy I want you to show this guy how great this vehicle is, and how sorry you are for not listening to him, when he first requested the test drive. The customer leans over to Tacky, listen I think that young man needs some sleep. His eyes are really bloodshot. Tacky just nods and turns away as Jimmy leads the customer out to drive the car.

Franklin gets driven in by his girlfriend and they both come to Tim's office. Tim shakes hands with Franklin and gets introduced to his girlfriend. I have to ask you franklin why did you want to know the location of the closest Clark station. My girlfriend's car is low on gas and I am going to lend her my Clark gas card to get home. Tim gives a sigh of relief. Ok let's get this deal done, and escorts them to Tricky's office.

Jimmy and the customer come back after the test drive and pull up outside Tacky's office. As their walking past Tacky's office Tacky stops them and motions both of them to step into his office. Sir I'm sorry I didn't get your name when I spoke with you. I'm Melvin Dupree and what's your name? Hi Melvin I'm John Bennett and I'm pleased to meet you. Come on and sit down, would you like something to drink, water, beer or maybe a shot. Thanks Melvin that's very kind of you, I will have a shot of whiskey, with some water. Meanwhile Jimmy is thinking the old man is going crazy.

Why is he treating this guy like he's some big shot. Ok John I can discount the Land cruiser a little. Are you trading in that pickup? John laughs, hell no I bought that truck thirty years ago. I drive that out into the fields and it really gets abused, but it's held up after all these years, that's why I'm looking at a new vehicle from your dealership. Tacky writes down a price on a piece of paper and slides it over to John. John looks at it for a few moments, then asks is this price including tax. Tacky shakes his head no, with the price of the Land Cruiser I can't afford to absorb the tax. There's not enough profit to do that. John downs the shot of whiskey and says Melvin pour us both a shot I think we have a deal. Tacky pours two shots they clink glasses and down the shots. Jimmy escort John to the finance office to do the paperwork. As their walking to Tricky's office Jimmy says John how can you afford to buy such an expensive vehicle. John smiles I sold my crops this morning and deposited ninety grand into my account. Jimmy's almost floored I didn't think farmers made that kind of money. John laughs, you've been watching too many old movies.

Can you get someone to clean that SUV up for me. No problem John I'll get that done for you. Jimmy drives the land cruiser to the wash rack, and tells Glen to clean it up for delivery. As jimmy is going back to the showroom Tacky grabs him and drags him into his office. Listen you little ass hole, you never tell a customer that he can't afford to buy something from our lot. I'm sorry dad when I saw how he was dressed and the truck he was driving I just assumed he didn't have any money. So Jimmy does he have any money. Yes Dad he told me he just put ninety grand into his checking account. Listen Jimmy you can't tell how wealthy a man is by how he's dressed. I want you to drive his old truck and follow him home. Hey dad can't you get a porter to drive it to his house. No Jimmy my porters are more valuable than you at this time. So get your ass out there and follow him home

29

Sly and Myrna

About a mile down the road at Georges Auto Repair Sly McGee is looking at his engine hanging from an overhead hoist. There's a hole in the side of the block big enough for Tom Brady to throw his cell phone through, and there's a connecting rod hanging out of the hole. George Tenopoulos is shaking his head. Mr. McGee did you ever change the oil in the car. Sly looks at George Tenopoulos, you mean you have to put oil in these cars. Mr. McGee I can't believe you drove this car and never put oil in it. Can I call you George? George shakes his head yes. Well George is there a warranty on this car. Mr. McGee not the way it's been abused. Ok George get me an estimate on how much it will cost to be fixed. Sly walks back into the office and tells his girlfriend Myrna to hike her skirt up so George might be distracted and give them a better price. Myrna just groans, why me. I have to always do your dirty work. George comes into the office after cleaning the gunk off his hands, sits down at his desk and gives Myrna's legs the once over.

Myrna crosses her legs and then crosses them the other way giving George a better view. Sly smiles Myra knows her stuff. After several minutes George adds up all the parts and labor. Ok Mr. McGee it's going to cost sixty five hundred plus tax. Sly is floored is there some way we can get the price down. George shakes his head. This is the best

I can do. Sly motions towards Myrna. George laughs your girlfriend is cute but I can't feed my family on her. Listen just stick the engine back in and I'll think of some way of getting it out of here. Ok Mr. McGee Right now I have one hundred and fifty in towing, four hundred to pull the motor out and another four hundred to put it back in. So you're going to have to come up with nine hundred and fifty. If you leave your car here I charge fifty bucks a day storage. Sly is beside himself, Hey George the sign outside says free estimates. George just gives Sly a cold stare. If you wanted a tune up or a tire repair I can give you a free estimate, all which stops when I have to tow you in. Sly thinks for several moments. Can I steer the car with no engine? George gives Sly a puzzled look. I suppose you could steer the car with no engine, but where are you going to go. Sly tells George to put the car out front and he wants George to push it down the street to Dupree's dealership. But first George we have to change clothes. Sly digs some clothes out of the trunk and Myrna and Sly Go into the bathroom to change.

When they come out Sly is dressed as a priest and Myrna is dressed as a nun. They both hop in the car and tell George to give them a push. Not so fast sunny boy I want the five hundred and fifty you owe me. Sly sheepishly smiles, I thought you keeping the motor was a good exchange for the charges. George shakes his head, the motor is a piece of garbage, now give me the money or you go nowhere. Ok, ok, Sly reaches into his pocket and pulls out a roll of money, and gives George the five fifty.

Jimmy is just getting back from delivering the car when he sees this car come careening in off the street and pull up in front of the showroom. A priest and nun get out of the car. Jimmy thinks, has the word gotten out about giving the nun's a free car, so they'll all come over to get one. As they enter the showroom, Tim approaches them and asks how he can be of service? Myrna sizes Tim up and thinks I know how he could be of service to me. I could be a child molester. Myrna starts to giggle. Sly looks at her as if she has lost her mind.

Tim introduces himself to Sly And Myrna. Sly shakes Tim's hand, then tells him he wants to trade in their late model car for something sportier. Myrna takes Tim's hand in both of her hands, rubbing them she says Tim your hands are so warm. Sly breaks in, of course their warm he just got through shaking my hand. Tim inquires why a priest would want a sporty car. Sly replies were not catholic, our order is more into living a good life. Sly looks over at the Sentenal 455 convertible, I like that car how much would it cost after we trade in my late model. They follow Tim to his office to get an appraisal card filled out. This time Myrna positions herself so that her gown is pulled to the side revealing a lot of leg and thigh. Tim gets the keys from Sly and tells him that we need to drive the car to properly appraise it. Sly retorts it's a late model why would you need to drive it. Tim tells him its company policy, he has to abide by it. Sly hands Tim the keys, thinking fast he turns to Myrna. You can't let them drive the car so get your ass out there. Myrna says what can I do? Sly smiles, use that charm you were showing Tim just a few minutes ago.

Tim approaches Jimmy. Hey Jimmy can you appraise that car for a trade in, or should I give it to Tacky. Jimmy grabs the appraisal card. I can appraise it just as good as the old man. In the back of his mind remembering the ass chewing he got on the last deal. Jimmy is walking toward the car when he almost gets knocked over by Myrna. She opens the driver's door kneels down on the front seat. As she is kneeling down she pulls up her gown to reveal she is not wearing panties. Jimmy gets a full blown moon. Myrna then turns over and leaning back toward the passenger seat to retrieve something from the glove box. Gives Jimmy a complete front view. Myrna sits up and smiles, I hope I didn't offend you. Jimmy's face is beet red, you're not wearing underwear. Of course not why do you think they call us nuns. Myrna see's the smile on Jimmy's face suddenly change to a look of anguish. Myrna thinks what the hell, I still have a great body. She doesn't understand that for a split second Jimmy's mind goes back to Sister Mary and he almost chokes, with a mental image of a naked ninety year old Sister Mary. Excuse me Sister Myrna I have to drive this car. Myrna puts her arms around Jimmy. This car is in excellent condition. Look at the low miles, as she is rubbing against Jimmy. Jimmy thinks I'm going to hell, but so what this feels good. Your right Sister Myrna the car looks good to me. Jimmy gives the card back to Tim. The car is in great shape, just do the deal.

Tony's been checking this deal out and wondering why the sister Myrna didn't want Jimmy to drive the car. Tim puts a deal together for

Sly and Sly approves with no hesitation. So Tim escorts Sly and Myrna to Tricky's office. After introductions Tricky runs a credit bureau on Sly. Tony has stationed himself outside of Tricky's office, and hears the laugh from Tricky as he prints out the credit report. Tricky shouts, hey Tony come in here. As Tony's walking in Tricky hands him the credit report. Tony glances at the report and hears Tricky snaps his fingers and say's a one and a two and a three. They both begin singing unfinancible that's what you are. unfinancible you can't buy the car. It's regrettable so unfinancible, unfinancibly true Both Tricky and Tony are laughing so hard their both bent over. Tony recovers telling Tricky, don't we have one of those loans available for this con man. Sly is beside himself. I don't understand what's wrong with my credit. Tricky puts his hand on Sly's shoulder. My friend you couldn't buy yesterday's newspaper on credit. How much money do you have in your pocket? Sly can't believe it he's being shaken down. I think I have about a couple of grand. Great say's Tricky, ok let's get the deal started. Meanwhile Sister Myrna is eyeing up Tim. Maybe Tim you could show me the car that Reverend Sylvester is buying. Tim smiles sure I can show you the car. As their walking out to the new car lot, Sister Myrna leans over and gives Tim a small kiss on his cheek. You know Tim I have an itchy pussy. Tim has a bewildered look on his face, is that car made in Korea? Myrna giggles, you are so clueless, and why don't you show me that camper at the back of the lot. Tim stops and turns to Myrna I thought you wanted to see the car that the reverend is buying. Myrna thinks I can't believe how dumb this kid is. Tim I might want to buy this for myself. Ok sister I don't understand how a nun can afford to buy a camper. Myrna gives Tim a short laugh, if I want it don't worry I can get all the money I need. So quit standing there and get the keys. Tim runs back to get the keys for the camper, and is thinking oh boy I might score another sale. As soon as Tim gets back with the keys and opens the door, Myrna pushes him inside. She turns, closes the door and locks it. Moments later all you can hear is Tim exclaim, oh boy' oh wow' OH WOOOW.

Back in Tricky's office Sly is getting grilled by Tony. Listen Reverend Sylvester or how about Sly because you thought you could pull one over on us. I know that car is missing the motor and you didn't want Jimmy to try and drive it. I don't know how you got it here. It doesn't matter we will get you financed, but it's going to cost you. Tricky starts to smile knowing he's about to make a killing. Tricky what's the highest rate we can charge him? Tony it's about forty eight percent. Ok tricky add on paint and fabric protection. An extended warranty, plus croak and choke. [An insurance policy that pays off the car if the person financing dies. Or if the person gets sick or in an accident and can't make the payments.] Sly shakes his head I won't be able to make the payments, if they're so high. Sly you probably won't make the payments anyway. Tricky looks at Tony what about the trade? Jimmy is giving top dollar for it, should I change it. Tricky leave it like it is I need to teach that kid a lesson. Finally as their finishing up Myrna appears with smiling Tim. Sly gives Myrna a questioning look. Myrna says what' he was just going over everything with me. Sly says yea I'll bet he was going over everything. After they leave Tacky notices that there is oil dripping from the trade parked in front of the showroom. He pages Nick to the showroom. Hey Nick get the keys and move that trade to the back of the lot and then clean up that oil. Nick gets the keys, goes out to the car. After several minutes he gets out and opens the hood, slams it and comes back to the showroom. Tacky's getting aggravated, Nick move that car. Listen boss the engines missing. Ok Nick I don't care if it's missing just move it. Boss I said the engines missing. Ok Nick do I have to move it myself. Boss you can't move it the engine is gone. Tacky runs out to the car, opens the hood, comes back inside and doesn't need the intercom as he starts to scream for Jimmy.

Back in Tacky's office Jimmy comes in with a dumb look on his face. Hey old man what do you want, I could hear you hollering all the way back in service. Tacky is trying to be very patient. Jimmy sit down I want to talk to you about how our business works. We need to make a profit if we're going to stay in business. I have the deal here on the sale to the reverend, and it looks like you appraised the trade. Jimmy nods yea I appraised it, what's the big deal, it was a really nice trade. Remember earlier today when you appraised the trade for my old buddy, and you were gone for a really long time. Jimmy smiles yea I remember that test drive. I wound up with a broken pair of sun glasses. Ok Jimmy did you drive the trade on this deal. Dad I drove it and it ran perfectly. Are you sure you drove it. Dad why would I lie I drove the car. Jimmy I don't think you drove the car because the engines missing. Dad it could have been missing but that doesn't mean I didn't drive it. Jimmy you have to be one hell of a great driver to drive a car with no engine. Jimmy almost falls off the chair. What do you mean it has no engine? Jimmy I don't know how the car got here, it doesn't have a motor. Now why didn't you appraise it? I'm sorry dad the nun that came here with the reverend, assured me that the car was in excellent condition. Listen Jimmy this deal is going to cost me about four grand to put a motor back in that car. Jimmy if you want to keep working here, you have to remember that everyone that walks through door is looking to score a great deal. So you have to keep on your toes and not anything interfere with your job. No matter how good looking a girl is or if you are offered something under the table, which includes sex. Do you understand me? Jimmy nods in affirmative, sorry dad it won't happen again.

Jimmy walks out of Tacky's office and sees Tim with a big smile on his face. What's up Tim. Jimmy I made a huge commission on that deal with the reverend, and I got screwed by the nun. Tim that's great I hope you had a good time with her. Whether you know it or not I also got screwed by the Nun.

Tim's Delivery

As Tim and Jimmy are talking, this young girl comes in with her mother and father. Tim confides to Jimmy that this girl has come in several times to try and sell ad space in a religious newsletter. She always looked like those church ladies with long dresses and no makeup with her hair pulled back, plus the large glasses. Jimmy starts to laugh, she doesn't look too bad now. Tim has to agree. Well Jimmy she must be thinking about buying a new car from the ones that I showed her. Tim walks over to greet them. He's trying to remember her name, when her mother says to Tim so you want to sell my sweet daughter Rosie a car. That's right Rosie's mother and what's your name and your husband. I'm Hannah and this big man is Volker. Tim shakes both their hands and feels some pain from Volker's handshake. Rosie goes over to the Econ 20 and tells her parents that this is the car she can afford. Her father looks at the sticker price and immediately asks Tim how much he can discount it. Tim explains that there is not much of a markup on these models, but he is sure that Rosie qualifies for the first time buyer discount. Volker grabs Tim's hand and again squeezes it hard, proclaiming she will take it. They all go into Tim's office to do the write up. Since the parents are going to cosign, they fill out the sales order. Tim takes them to Tricky's office. He tells them that he will get the car off the showroom floor and make sure everything is ok. Jimmy is helping Tim get the car off the floor and leans over to tease Tim. I don't think you're going to score like you did earlier. As Rosie comes out of Tricky's office, she tells Tim you are going to show me how everything works or I won't take the car home. Don't worry Rosie I will fill you in on everything. I hope so Tim I really want you to fill me in. Again Tim has that deer in the headlamp look. Rosie's parents leave because the sky is suddenly getting dark from a summer storm that's moving in. Just as Tim and Rosie start walking out to the car lot, where the car is parked, it starts to rain. Tacky walks over to the showroom window to join Jimmy as they watch Tim go over the accessories with Rosie. Moments later it starts to rain so hard that they are almost invisible to Tacky and Jimmy. Suddenly Tacky blurts out, Jimmy did you see what looks like someone's naked butt. Yea dad I think I saw something that looks like a naked butt. Oh my god I think I saw two legs up in the air. Jimmy shakes his head, dad I think the rain is playing tricks on us. Tacky is scratching his head, you are probably right. Just as fast as the storm started it rolls past, and as the rivulets of water roll off the car, the sun comes out. Tacky and Jimmy watch as Tim shakes hands with Rosie and gets out of the car. Tacky smiles, Jimmy you were right the rain was playing tricks on us. And then walks away back to his office. Tim walks in smiling. Jimmy can't help himself, and blurts out, you hit that didn't you. Tim puts his hands up in the air as if he didn't understand. I don't know what you're talking about. Jimmy starts laughing well I think you should zip up your pants. Tim gets a little red faced and pulls up the zipper.

Spoiled Brat

Earlier in the day a women and her daughter drove onto the new car lot and were looking at the land cruiser diamond edition that Tacky sold later. At that time Faruk walked out to see if he could be of assistance to the ladies. After several minutes Faruk shakes his head and walks back to the showroom. The girls stand around for several minutes and then get back into their car and drive away. Tacky was watching but didn't ask Faruk about what was happening. Because he figured the price probably was too high and they didn't want to pay that price. So as the evening starts the same car comes back to the new car lot with the girls, but a man is driving. Tacky comes out of his office and motions for Faruk to go and greet the people. Faruk tells Tacky I don't want to talk to those people. Have someone else take care of them. Tacky gives Faruk a cold stare, when did you start becoming so good you can't take care of the customers. Faruk raises his hands in a sign of surrender, ok I'll go out and talk to them. Tacky watches as Faruk walks over to the man and puts out his hand to shake hands with him. The girl says something and the man pushes Faruk's hand away. The three of them walk toward the showroom. As they come through the showroom door Tacky comes out of his office to find out what is going on. The man walks right up to Tacky, puts his finger in Tacky's chest and in a threatening voice says I want to see the manager. Tacky grabs the man's finger pushing it away from his chest and says I'm the owner, what can I do for you. My name is George Sanfort I own a large parts house on the west side. You probably heard of me, this is my wife Penny and my daughter Mindy. Tacky smiles, no I've never heard of you, but what is going on? George barks at Tacky I want that salesman fired he insulted my daughter. Tacky knows from experience that Faruk never insults anyone, in fact Faruk is always smooth as silk. How did my salesman insult your daughter? Mindy pipes in, I told him that I wanted to buy that Land Cruiser. He said it is very expensive, are you sure you want to spend that kind of money. I told him I can buy anything I put my mind to. He smiled and said he has the same problem with his own daughter. When she wants something she just earns the money to get it. I told him, he is just a salesman and his daughter couldn't compare to me. Besides he comes from some third world country, and doesn't speak good English. So I was insulted. Penny chimes in, what is this country coming to when a stupid salesman thinks he is as good as us. George smiles at Tacky, I bet your daughter wouldn't put up with this either. Tacky's smile slowly fades from his face. I don't have a daughter I have a son, but if I had a daughter that was like your daughter I would have kill the bitch. Now I would like you to take that stupid skinny ass wife of yours and that spoiled bitch of a daughter and get off my lot. You have insulted my salesman and insulted me. George begins to make a fist, and says I don't have put up with this shit. Tacky smiles you're in my store and if you start something you will regret it. George thinks for a moment and says I'm going to call the better business bureau and have you written up in all the papers. Mindy grabs her dad's arm daddy come on hit him he insulted me. Beat him up. Tacky says that's right daddy beat me up. But only if you can. George pushes her hand away. Shut up you stupid kid, look what you got me into. With that they all storm out. Tacky turns around and see's the entire sales force standing there looking at him. Then they all start cheering and clapping. Tacky grabs Faruk, listen I want to commend you for what I put you through. Faruk smiles you just made my day and probably my year

Tacky's Ex and Judy

Tacky goes back into his office, grabs a glass, gets some ice from the fridge, and pours himself a large amount of scotch. Just as he's chilling out he sees an old Volkswagen limp onto the lot and park just outside his office window. Tacky thinks I can't believe that thing is still running. Both doors open and out pops his ex-wife Donna Dupree and the driver who looks like a German army runaway. Donna drags the guy into Tacky's office. Okay Donna why do I have the privilege of your visit. Tacky I was worried about Jimmy and came to see him. Donna who do you think you're kidding. If you want to see Jimmy He's probably hanging out somewhere. The only time you pay me a visit is when you want something. Today I'm not in the giving mood. Besides normally you wouldn't be caught dead in that old piece of shit car. The German puts his hand up in protest. That is not a piece of shit as you would call it. That is a fine German engineered vehicle, and will be on the road for many more years. All right it may be on the road but your feet will be hanging out the bottom. Donna who is this refuge from the Third Reich. Tacky let me introduce Hans Geoble he is my personal trainer. Tacky I thought maybe you could help Hans get into something newer. Donna, Hans is getting into you, I really don't want him getting into me. Tacky, come on, Hans needs a car, can't you help him. Donna I give you enough money, maybe you could give him some, so he can buy his own car. Donna looks like she's going to say something, so Tacky puts up his hand to silence her. Listen Donna, as usual I'll help you out, go and grab Jimmy so he can find something used for Hans. Hey Hans have you been able to put Donna's legs over her head? Ya I do that several times a day. Hans, Donna only does that when she wants to welcome some guy, it works better than perfume. Donna while you and Hans are looking around I want to remind you Jimmy is going home with you tonight. Tacky I thought Jimmy was going to stay with you now that he graduated. Listen Donna I've been paying child support all these years, so you can take care of him. Besides he screwed up another new car. I'm not going to let him drive another new car until he pays me back for the damage on the one he just messed up. Tacky where is Hans going to stay if Jimmy comes home with me. Tacky laughs, He's going to stay in your bedroom like he always does. Tacky gets on the intercom and calls Charlie to his office. Charlie comes in, what's up Mr. Tacky. Charlie find Donna and that guy, get his keys and get that piece of shit moved away from my office. I don't want to give the dealership a bad name. Charlie smiles okay boss I'll put it out by the junk pile.

Judy comes to visit

Jimmy starts showing Donna and Hans some used cars while filling her in on all the work he had to do just too graduate college. Jimmy's getting bored because Hans is asking all kinds of technical questions about the cars he's looking at, that Jimmy has no answers for. As their walking around the lot, Jimmy hears a familiar voice calling his name.

Judy almost runs down Hans when she sees Jimmy. She jumps out of the car runs up and throws her hands around Jimmy kissing him all over his face. Oh Jimmy I missed you so much, I'm so happy you are back in town. Guess what, as she says that, there's this loud barking from her car, I got this wonderful little dog. She reaches into the car and brings out a small white poodle. Jimmy this is Honey Bee, isn't he beautiful. Judy holds the dog close to her very large and supple breasts. Jimmy reaches over to pet the dog and gets nipped by Honey Bee. Damn what's the matter with that dog? Honey Bee the dog, thinks those are my breasts don't even come near them. Judy says hello to Donna and Donna introduces Judy to Hans. Hans looks at Judy and then looks at Donna, and thinks why am I dining on flank steak when I could be munching on filet mignon. Young lady it's a pleasure to meet you, I am a personal trainer and could help you get in better shape. Suddenly the veins begin to swell on Donna's face and neck. Judy' if Hans is going to give you some personal training, it will be out in the alley with all his belongings. Hans smiles Donna sweetie, I was only trying to be helpful. Donna points to an older trade in and tells Jimmy that car is good enough for Hans. Jimmy smiles ok mom I'll have Charlie switch the plates. Han's is happy because it's an older BMW, a lot newer than what he was driving. Jimmy and Judy go inside to Tacky's office. Hey dad look who's here, it's Judy. Tacky stands up and gives Judy a hug. I'm so happy you're here maybe you can help this six year waste of an education become a little less stupid. Jimmy turns to Judy with a please help me expression on his face. Honey Bee jumps out of Judy's arms and runs over to Tacky and leaps into Tacky's lap. Jimmy's upset, dad I think that dog is vicious he tried to bite me when I was going to kiss Judy. Tacky's thinking if I were that dog and could lick those melons I would kill anyone who came near them. Charlie heads back to the service department to see if he can help Dan finish up and deliver some cars.

Mrs. McHenry

Dan's finishing up and closing out tickets when Mrs. McHenry sneaks up on him and grabs him by his rear end, causing him to jump and swear. He turns around and. I'm sorry I didn't see you Mrs. McHenry. She smiles, Dan I just had to grab your ass, it looks so good. Dan starts to blush. Dan I'm sorry I gave you such a bad time, I stopped at the cashiers and she told me you gave me a real nice discount, and some coupons for future repairs. So I want to apologize and maybe I can do something to make it up to you. By the way you can call me Tiny Lilly. Dan says Tiny Lilly. How did you get that name? I was the smallest girl in the family. Dan nods his head I understand, and thinks your four hundred pounds, how big are your sisters. Dan would you walk me to the car and I'll show you how I'm going to thank you. Dan doesn't know what to do, and like a miracle Charley appears. Tiny Lilly I would love to take you to your car, I'm just to busy, Charley will escort you. Charley gives Dan a mean look, Ok mamm Lets go. After Charley sends Mrs. McHenry off Tacky calls him to his office. Ok Charley lets start shutting things down. Tim comes back to he show room and starts gulping down water. Charley laughs, are we a little dehidrated Tim. Charlie I thought I was going to pass out. This selling cars can almost kill someone. Charley starts checking cars to make sure their locked and closes the service doors. Tacky leaves for home and tells charley he has to come in early tomorrow to get a car ready for a charity drawing. Charley thinks why don't I just live here.

He goes to Tacky's office and grabs a bottle of brandy, pours himself a nice glass full, sits down in Tacky's chair and calls Edna to pick him up. About fifteen minutes later and two glasses downed Edna shows up. He drives to the main gate, closes and locks it. Edna looks at him, Charley you look tired. Edna I'm seventy years old, dam right I'm tired. Edna gives him a nice kiss and says I got this great steak I'm going to make for you. Charley smiles, gives her a little kiss on her cheek. Thanks honey, but I'm getting to old for this shit. Let's go.

Printed in the United States
by Baker & Taylor Publisher Services